Also by GUS TAVO

HUNT THE MOUNTAIN LION
ILLUSTRATED BY BRINTON TURKLE

A Borzoi Book for Young People
PUBLISHED BY ALFRED A. KNOPF

The Buffalo are Running

THE BUFFALO

ARE RUNNING

by GUS TAVO

Illustrated by E. F. MILLER

ALFRED A. KNOPF: NEW YORK

1960

FOR
Susanne, Craig, Melissa, Elizabeth, and Taylor

L. C. Catalog card number 60–11421

THIS IS A BORZOI BOOK, PUBLISHED BY ALFRED A. KNOPF, INC.

FIRST EDITION

Contents

The Buffalo are Running

Back Home in Missouri

1

The boy came whistling down the path from the cabin, an ax over his shoulder. Beside the wood-pile he stopped and lowered the ax to the ground. Slowly his eyes swept the hillside. Spring was coming. The maple buds were bursting out pink. There was a pale green lace of new leaves on the old oaks. The ground felt alive and springy under his boots. Wild violets were blooming white and yellow and blue under their wide green leaves. From the old hickory at the foot of the hill came the rat-tat-tat of a redheaded woodpecker. The boy stretched his arms wide, breathing in the smells of spring.

Stooping, he set a stick of firewood against the chopping block. His hands were big on the wood, but deft. His shoulder blades stuck out thin and sharp under the homespun shirt. There was still the smooth roundness of boyhood to his face, a soft curve to his lips.

He straightened up, pushing impatiently at the yellow forelock fallen across his forehead. Sunlight glinted on the ax. The blade bit cleanly into the wood, halving the stick neatly.

From the top of the hill came a woman's voice. "David! Donald David Duncan!"

The boy grinned. "Down here, Grandma," he shouted.

His grandmother came swiftly down the path, holding her long calico skirt high over her boots, her apron strings fluttering. She was as straight and slender as a girl. She had the same deep blue eyes that her grandson had, but hers were netted with fine laugh lines. Her long white hair, combed severely back, escaped its knot in rebellious curls. The stubborn line of mouth and chin

[4]

was softened by dimples in both cheeks.

"David Duncan," she panted. "If you cut one more stick of kindling, you're not going. The woodshed is crammed full of firewood. I couldn't use that much in five years, let alone one."

David sat down on a stump, chopping at the turf with his ax. "Guess I'm just taking out my waiting on the wood," he said ruefully. "If Bart doesn't come for me pretty soon, I reckon I'll bust wide open."

She sank down on a log at his feet. "I still can't rest easy in my mind for you to start out to Oregon with Bart Clements, David. Not with your Uncle Andrew despising him so. I hate to think what Andrew'll say."

"I only hope Uncle Andrew's alive to say it, Grandma. Down at the store folks are worrying that the whole company could have been wiped out down in Texas. It's over eight months, now, and not a word from any of them."

"I'll never believe Andrew Duncan's been killed in war!" his grandmother said hotly. "Never! Andrew'll get back. You mark my words."

"Anyway, Uncle Andrew would be the last man to hold me back from going west, not when everybody who can rustle a wagon and oxen is heading out."

"Andrew would have held you back from going with Bart. Andrew never did trust Bart. That's what worries me. I must have been out of my mind when I signed the paper for you to go with him. Trusting your life to him. He never would have hired you, only he knows you've got your poor pa's rifle. I wish Bart'd never seen you win that shooting match."

The boy's face hardened. "Bart was my only chance. I couldn't have gone, if you hadn't signed. I haven't forgotten how I walked all the way to Independence or how the wagon bosses there just laughed at me. Said they were hiring men, not boys."

"They showed good sense."

"Look, Grandma, Bart's paying me good wages to herd cavvy to Oregon. We can use that money. Besides, men who come back from the Oregon Trail say a fellow with a good rifle can pile up a stake for himself with buffalo robes. That's what I aim to do." He knelt down and put his arms around her. "I've got to be the man of this family now," he said unsteadily.

Gently she pulled away from him. "You're just a boy. I know you're a crack shot, but buffalo. That's a man's job. Besides, there'll be Injuns to steal the horses, and blizzards to give you frostbite, and flash floods to wash the wagons away, and—"

"Grandma! I know all that's so, but plenty of folks are making it all the time. Look around you here, Grandma. We've got a wagon, but we don't have any horse to pull it. We've got us a good cabin and farm, but we don't have any cows. You saw the stack of buffalo robes Bart brought back last trip. You know how much money he got for them. A fellow can't make a living out of squirrel skins and rabbit. I'm fairly itching to go after buffalo."

"Buffalo! Oregon Trail! Buffalo! That's all you can think of," she cried angrily, then softened at the troubled look in his eyes. "I wouldn't worry so, if I could just go with you," she whispered fiercely.

David sighed. "If only you could. But us, with no money for oxen or a grubstake—besides, the Oregon Trail would sure be too hard on you, Grandma."

Her blue eyes flashed. "I'll be all of fifty my next birthday," she said tartly, "and I'm still handy with a rifle." Tears flooded her eyes. "And here I have to sit with my hands folded."

"If only I could figure out some way—" the boy's voice trailed off hoarsely.

She wiped her eyes with the corner of her apron, straightening her shoulders determinedly. "Well, there isn't any," she said flatly. "We've

[7]

been over and over it enough times to know that. I don't know why I'm fretting over you, anyhow. You're a Duncan. There's no use arguing with a Duncan, once his mind's made up."

"Oh, Grandma, I'm going to miss you so!" the boy said miserably.

"I know," she said thickly. "It'll be lonesome here in the cabin." Angrily she swiped at her tears again with the back of her hand. "Here," she told him, fumbling in the pocket of her apron, "here, you take this with you, David."

David took the little Testament that she thrust at him, turning it awkwardly in his big hands. "I never saw this before," he said wonderingly.

"It was your ma's, God rest her soul. It's right you should have it now. You read it every single day. Long as you listen to the words, the good Lord will take care of you."

On the Oregon Trail

2

The long train of covered wagons crawled with agonizing slowness up the steep slope. Behind lay the sun-scorched prairie. Ahead stretched a desolate wasteland, eroded, barren, with chalky buttes, stark mesas, grotesque, tortuous rock formations.

The sun blazed down from a cloudless sky.

Tall buffalo grass bent flat beneath the searing wind that howled around the wagons and drowned out the crack of bull whips, the hoarse gees and haws shouted at the plodding oxen.

The trail was a wide swath of sunbaked ruts cut deep by a thousand wagon wheels. Oxen slipped and stumbled as they strained against their yokes. Wagons jounced, lurching from side to side. Clouds of dust rolled back from under their wheels.

A hundred feet behind the wagons, the straggling cavvy of horses and mules and oxen caught the brunt of the dust. The herders, a boy on a black mule and an old white-bearded man on a scrawny pinto, rode slumped in their saddles, kerchiefs knotted across their faces.

Dully the boy gazed out of red-rimmed eyes at the scattered black circles of dead campfires, the broken wagon wheels, the bleached skeletons of oxen and horses which lay along the trail. He jumped, startled, when the old man pushed his pinto up alongside the mule.

"Dave," the old man cried hoarsely, "you see that tallest rock pile a couple miles up there ahead? That's Scott's Bluff, Dave. Not more'n fifty miles from there on into Fort Laramie."

David squinted through the dust. The bluff

towered high over the other buttes. Its sheer cliffs were slashed by countless rocky ledges, outjutting like bastions on a fortress.

"Spooky," the boy muttered, "like something out of a nightmare, Amos."

The old man snorted. "Spooky or not, the trail gets back to the Platte River at the foot of that bluff. First thing I aim to do when we get there is wade out to one of those little islands in the river and set down under a tree and soak my feet."

"I can see Bart letting you do that," the boy jeered.

Amos chuckled. "Well, anyways, I'm powerful glad to see Scott's Bluff. The going'll get easier now."

David laughed. "We're six hundred miles out from Independence, Amos, and I'll bet you've promised me six hundred times things will start getting easier."

"They will, too, Dave, mark my words. Why don't you ride on ahead? A drink of water will perk you up. I can manage the cavvy by myself."

"And give Bart another chance to cuss me out for letting the Injuns steal that mule the other night? Not me."

"Dave, don't let Bart get you all riled up. He's

wagon boss. As long as we're herding cavvy, the wagon boss is going to blame us for everything that goes wrong with the stock."

"But, Amos, I swear I drove that picket stake in plenty deep!"

"I know you did, Dave. Bart, he likely knows it, too. I've seen a lot of wagon bosses in my time. Reckon Bart's about the toughest I ever come across. Seems like he ain't happy unless he's blaming something on somebody."

"Grandma warned me Bart was like that," the boy muttered, but so low that Amos did not hear.

They rode on in silence. The trail was a hard uphill pull, winding in and around ghostly shapes of chalky rock that towered over them like weird sentinels. By the time the cavvy reached the top of the high ridge, the first dozen wagons were already down on the valley floor, crawling toward the gray ribbon of river over against the bluff.

The cavvy, smelling water, started down the trail at a trot.

"Come on, Dave! Get out front and hold them back!"

They pushed their mounts in and around the thirsty stock. Out in front they began to zigzag back and forth, slowing the cavvy to a walk.

"Bart'd blow his top, was we to let them stampede on this slope," Amos growled. "Get back there, you ornery ox!" He jerked off his battered old hat and fanned it angrily.

The last wagon was halfway across to the river by the time they reached the valley floor. When the trail flattened out, Amos gave up on holding the cavvy back.

"Even Bart couldn't work no miracle now," he said sourly, as horses and mules and oxen broke for the river. "Run, you dumb critters! Even that muddy water will taste good. Come on, Dave, hurry up that mule."

David kicked the mule into a lope. "Amos," he hollered, "look! The wagons are forming a circle by the river."

"Danged if they ain't! Wonder what Bart's up to?"

"I don't know, but he's waiting for us up there beside the trail."

Bart Clements's big bay stallion pranced nervously as they rode up. David stared sullenly at the wagon boss. Bart was a big man, and brawny, with swarthy face and heavy black beard. His eyes were small and black and set deep under frowning brows.

"You two took your own sweet time getting here," he snarled.

"Didn't want to heat up the stock this early in

the morning," Amos said amicably. "How come the wagons are making circle, Bart?"

"Those greenhorn settlers have driven their oxen till they're worn out," Bart growled. "We're laying up till tomorrow. You two round up the cavvy and hobble them out on that flat between the wagons and the river. And when I say hobble, I mean hobble! You lose us one more head of stock, and you'll both herd cavvy afoot."

"It was me that staked out that mule, Bart," David said steadily. "Amos didn't have anything to do with it."

"When I hired you to herd cavvy, I figured you was smart enough to stake out a mule," Bart snarled, "even if you were Andrew Duncan's kin. It looks like you ain't. I'm not going to warn you but this one time." He wheeled the bay stallion. "Soon as you finish with the cavvy, rustle up plenty of firewood," he shouted over his shoulder, then spurred the bay toward the circling wagons.

It took them the better part of an hour to hobble the cavvy and another hour to gather enough firewood to win a dour nod from Bart Clements.

"I'm scouting ahead with Cal Tanner and Roy Edwards," he growled to Amos. "See to it Dave don't have a chance to loaf."

By then a dozen fires were crackling inside the

circle of wagons. Women bustled about, cooking dinner for their families. Children chased in and out, laughing and shouting.

Amos and David stowed their saddles and rifles under the big supply wagon. While David built up a fire and put on the coffeepot, Amos deftly mixed biscuits and tucked them inside a blackened Dutch oven. David stretched out by the fire and watched Amos rake hot coals up over the oven.

"Used our last cup of flour," the old man grunted. "Have to make out with sowbelly until we hit Fort Laramie."

"Sowbelly's all right by me," David said lazily. "Anyway, Cal Tanner says we may see buffalo any day now. I'm fairly itching to kill me a buffalo."

Amos sat down with a tired grunt. "Running buffalo takes a good horse, Dave, with plenty know-how. You ain't never going to get close to buffalo with that mule Bart leaves you ride."

"Fat chance I have getting a horse, with Bart kicking me around just because he hates my Uncle Andrew," David said gloomily.

Amos leaned back on one elbow, squinting up at the sky. "Injuns got the best buffalo horses," he said absently. "Buffalo runners, they call them. Those horses will run straight into a herd of buffalo. You never seen nothing like the way they can dodge a wounded bull."

"Only thing I might trade for a horse is my Pa's rifle," David told him, "and without the rifle a horse wouldn't do me any good."

All at once Amos sat up. "See that eagle flying way up there? Look, circling over the bluff."

"Where? Oh, I see it."

"Did you know a dozen tail feathers from a eagle be the price of a Injun buffalo runner?"

"A dozen feathers?" David stared at the eagle until it vanished behind the bluff. "That wouldn't be any trick."

Amos laughed. "Why do you reckon Injuns be ready to trade a good horse for them? They ain't so easy to come by."

David flopped over on his stomach and peered out under the wagon at the stretch of plain beyond the camp. Here and there the bleached skull of a buffalo gleamed dully in the sun. Chalky bones scattered the prairie grass.

"Even with the grass eaten down all along the trail, Amos, this valley must be good buffalo hunting ground. I never saw so many bones."

"They come here, all right, on account of the water, Dave, but this valley's poison for running buffalo."

"Why?"

"Look out there on the slope. Those dadblasted prairie dogs have taken the whole valley. It'd be murder to run a horse over those holes."

David studied the hundreds of small dirt mounds that dotted the slope. Here and there a fat little prairie dog sat beside a mound, nose pointed toward the sky. The boy grinned.

"They're cunning little varmints, Amos."

The old man did not answer. He was leaning forward, peering intently out under the wagon.

"Dave," he whispered suddenly, "is your rifle loaded?"

"Sure. Why? What is it?"

"See that shadow drifting along over the dogs? That eagle is back. He's fixing to grab him a dog."

David snatched up his gun, and they scrambled out under the wagon. The eagle was directly overhead. Suddenly he folded his wings close to his body and plummeted earthward. There was a whistling swish of wings as he braked. Then he struck with a swoop and zoomed up into the air, a prairie dog dangling from his talons. At that instant David's rifle cracked.

"Missed!" the boy cried. Scowling, he watched the eagle fade smaller and smaller and finally vanish behind the bluff.

"You see, now, it ain't so easy," Amos told him. "Dave! Where you going?"

David had dived back under the wagon. He came up with his shoulder pouch and powder horn. "I'm going after that eagle," he said grimly, slipping the pouch strap over his shoulder.

"But that eagle's got his nest atop the bluff, Dave."

"I've climbed worse bluffs back home," David told him. "I aim to get me twelve tail feathers."

He set off at a jogging trot toward the bluff.

"Dave!" Amos hollered after him. "Wait!"

The boy halted. "What for?" he called impatiently, turning back.

Amos had his head inside the supply wagon. He fished out a coil of sturdy rope. "Take this," he said. "You can't get nowhere among those cliffs without a rope."

David looped the rope over his shoulder. "Much obliged, Amos. I'll be back before dark. If Bart gets here first, don't tell him where I've gone."

He set off toward the bluff. The old man stood watching. Slowly he shook his head.

The Nest on the Ledge

3

The approach to the bluff was a steep incline of white sand. David sank ankle deep with each step. By the time he reached the base, he was panting. Salty, stinging sweat trickled down his brow. He leaned back against the cool rock and pulled off his battered old hat, grateful for the breeze that lifted his hair.

Wiping the sweat from his face with his sleeve, he stepped back and scanned the face of the bluff. The eagle's nest wasn't likely on this side. Both times the big bird had flown over the bluff, then vanished beyond.

The boy clapped his hat on his head and started out around the face of the bluff, stumbling and sliding in the caving sand. When he was out of sight of the Platte and the wagon train he rested a moment, then worked his way around a jutting point. On the far side he stumbled on what he sought—a wind-eroded cliff cut by ledges and crevices.

He loaded his rifle, ramming ball and wadding home carefully, then slung the gun across his shoulder and started up. It was easy, at first. He scrambled up from ledge to ledge, searching out toeholds in cracks, jumping for handholds on jutting rocks, pulling himself up, sprawling on narrow ledges, fighting for breath.

He glanced down once. The sight made him hug the ledge where he lay. Far below the prairie stretched away in a fuzzy blend of grays and greens. He took a long, steadying breath.

At that instant a shadow passed over the ledge. David risked a quick glance up. In the sky directly overhead the eagle soared with outstretched wings, gliding down, down as it lost the wind, then catching a crosscurrent that carried it up until it was a speck in the sky.

The boy's heart thudded. The eagle was after more prey. That meant hungry eaglets in the nest and a parent bird that would return again and again with food. The boy scrambled to his knees, then eased up, hugging the face of the cliff. Slowly he inched along to the right until a crevice opened up and he began to climb.

He crawled out on top of the butte without knowing he had reached the end of his climb. He rested, panting, on hands and knees, shaking the sweat from his eyes. When he saw the flat plain of grass with its twisted, runty pines and cactus clumps, he dropped down on his stomach, gulping in the fresh cool air.

After a little he rolled over and sat up. He knew from the empty stretch of the butte top that he was above the eagle's nest.

"Only thing to do is work along the edge till I spot it," he said aloud. He got up and stepped cautiously over to where the butte dropped away to the valley below. Slowly he worked his way along the rim, scanning the ledges on the face of the cliff.

All at once from directly beneath his feet David heard a loud squeal, followed by short shrill cries and the whir of beating wings. He froze. There was no mistaking that flapping of wings. He knelt and peered over. The sheer rock wall fell away straight to the floor of the prairie hundreds of feet below.

The boy held his breath, straining to hear. For a moment the only sound was the whine of wind around the bluff. Then the shrill squealing commenced again.

David stretched out on his stomach on the ground. Carefully he inched forward until his head hung over the rim of the precipice. He caught his breath. Fifteen feet below the overhang of the bluff was a wide ledge. At one end was a giant nest built of sticks. Two half-grown eaglets played inside, fighting over a branch torn from a pine. They had brown feathers and big yellow beaks. On the backs of their heads were golden-brown hackles.

The boy hugged the ground, heart pounding. Even if the big eagle returned to the nest, he could not shoot from the top of the butte. Carefully he studied the ridges and grooves that cut the cliff. Suddenly his eyes fastened on a spot thirty feet beyond the nest, where the bluff jutted out in a ragged promontory. Twenty feet below the top was a ledge. If he could reach it, he would have a clear shot at the nest.

David pushed back from the rim and jumped

to his feet. He raced down to the promontory, then stretched out again and studied the descent. "Thanks to old Amos, I can make it," he muttered aloud.

Quickly he sat up and slipped the coil of rope off over his head. Shaking it out, he made a slip-knot and fastened it securely to a jutting arm of rock that reached out directly over the ledge. He got up and threw his weight on the rope. The rock held firm. Gingerly he sat down on the edge of the cliff, legs swinging free. He eased over cautiously, dangling loose, body twisting slowly as the wind caught him.

Inch by inch he let the rope slip through his hands. His palms burned. He craned his head to one side, eyes on the ledge below. His toes touched it. He leaned face forward against the bluff, heart pounding. When he could breathe, he eased around. Only then did he realize his luck. The ledge stretched unbroken under the overhang of bluff all the way to the eagle's nest.

He was still clutching the rope. He let it go and slipped his rifle off his shoulder. Slowly he eased down until he sat facing the nest, back wedged against the face of the bluff. He glanced up at the sun.

"Must of taken me a couple of hours since I left Amos," he said aloud. His voice bounced hollowly off the cliff. Squirming into a more comfortable position, he checked his gun. Powder, wadding, ball, cap. Cocking the hammer, he settled back to wait.

He did not have long. The first warning he had was the shrill squeals of the eaglets as they suddenly began to bounce up and down in the nest. The boy glanced up at the sky. His breath caught. The big eagle was zooming across the prairie toward the bluff. With huge wings spread wide, it soared up over the bluff, then plummeted down toward the ledge. Almost upon the nest the eagle braked, head and wings up, tail spread, feet thrust forward. From its talons dangled the limp body of a prairie dog.

The eagle came down with a shaking thump inside the nest. The great beak flashed up with a fragment of furry skin and tossed it over the edge of the nest. The eaglets were too hungry to wait. With a loud beating of wings they crowded the parent eagle aside and fell upon the prey with ravenous squeals. Calmly the big eagle hopped up on the side of the nest and fell to preening its feathers.

David was breathing in shallow gasps. The eagle had not seen him. Slowly, soundlessly, the boy raised his rifle. Suddenly the eagle caught the glint of sunlight on metal. Its head jerked around. For a second blazing red eyes glared ferociously into the boy's. David's finger squeezed the trigger. The rifle cracked. The bullet caught the eagle through the neck. It dropped heavily into the nest.

David was trembling when he laid his rifle down and got up. Slowly he inched his way along the ledge toward the nest. As he crept close, the boy whistled with astonishment. The nest was at least eight feet across. It was built of long sticks as thick as his wrist. The entire nest was lined with prairie grass and green pine branches. What he could see of the floor was strewn with partly eaten prairie dogs, rabbits, and old bones. The boy's nose wrinkled at the stench.

The eaglets did not pause in their struggle over the bloody remains of the prairie dog when the boy leaned over the nest. Gingerly he grasped the legs of the dead eagle and heaved it out onto the ledge. He gave an involuntary shudder at the feathered legs, the big yellow feet, the toes with their curving, razor-sharp black talons. He knelt down. Carefully he spread the tail wide, his eyes sparkling at the glossy white feathers with their black tips.

It did not take him long to pluck the feathers. He worked swiftly knowing the second eagle might return at any moment. Stowing the feathers away in his pouch, he crept back along the ledge until he reached the rope. He picked up his rifle and slipped the strap over his shoulder.

At that moment the eaglets set up a loud, shrill squealing. David looked up. High overhead a big eagle soared, circling the bluff in wide, sweeping glides. David grinned. The eaglets would not go hungry, not with the other parent bird bringing them prey.

The boy reached for the rope and groped for a toehold on the face of the bluff. Hand over hand he pulled himself up, not daring to rest for fear of losing his grip on the rope. His lungs were bursting. The ache in his arms was unbearable. Just when he was beginning to despair of making the top, his hand touched the jutting rock. He clutched at it desperately, hung for a second, then made one last exhausted lunge and heaved himself over the rim.

He lay limp, face pressed against the grass, legs still outstretched over the bluff. When he could breathe, he inched forward until his whole body lay on firm ground. Only then did he roll over and sit up.

His hands were raw and bloody from the rope. Face and legs were scratched and bruised. His homespun britches had long tears from sharp rocks. But the boy did not care. Safe in his pouch were the dozen tail feathers, the price of a buffalo runner.

He unfastened the rope and coiled it, then set out down the rim at a jogging trot, searching for an easy way down. The sun hung low in the west. The shadows of the scrubby pines stretched long on the ground.

He had almost circled the butte when he came upon a stretch where the precipice eased out in a steep slope toward the prairie below. The boy went over the side, slipping and sliding, catching at bushes and runty pines, ending up at the bottom in an avalance of rocks and sand.

Quickly he took his bearings from the sun and set out around the butte, slogging through sand ankle deep. Minutes later he caught sight of the river. He hurried, stumbling and panting around a rocky promontory, then brought up short. Not a hundred yards away was the camp. Smoke from a dozen fires hung in layers over the wagons. He had made it.

David crawled under the supply wagon just as dusk touched the prairie. Amos was standing beside the fire. Across the leaping flames stood Bart Clements and Cal Tanner. David ducked back, but Bart had seen him.

"Come out from under that wagon!" Bart snarled.

David crawled out and stood up, slapping futilely at his filthy clothes.

"Where have you been?" the wagon boss roared.

David shot one glance at Amos. The old man shook his head. The boy looked back at the angry wagon boss.

"Hunting," he said in a low voice.

"Hunting!" Bart yelled furiously. "Did I hire you for a hunter? Did I? Answer me."

"No, sir," David muttered.

"Then why did you go?" Bart shouted.

"I didn't think you'd mind," David told him. "I'd done my chores, and I hadn't had a chance to hunt since—"

"So, the cavvy boy from Missouri thinks he's a hunter," Bart cut in mockingly, his voice a sneering purr. "Reckon you must take after that fancy hunter uncle of yours."

Cal Tanner, a rawboned giant of a man with rusty red hair and deceptively gentle gray eyes, shuffled his feet impatiently. "Leave the boy be, Bart," he growled. "He ain't done nothing bad. We got more important things to worry about."

Bart shot him a venomous look, which the giant met unflinchingly. Before his steady gaze,

Bart hesitated, half turned away, then swung back.

"With all that fancy Duncan hunting of yours," he sneered, "what'd you bring in? I don't see no game."

David let out his breath slowly. "I didn't get any," he admitted. "Didn't kill anything but one old eagle."

Bart's hard black eyes glittered. "Eagle? You bring in the tail feathers, you blockhead?"

"I brought them," David nodded.

Bart stretched out one hairy hand. "Let's have them."

David drew back. "They're mine! I killed the eagle."

"You were hunting on my time!" Bart screamed in sudden fury. "Hand over those feathers!"

David's face paled, but he met Bart's furious glare unflinchingly. "No," he said firmly. "I aim to trade them for a buffalo runner at Fort Laramie."

Bart took one menacing step forward, fist raised. "Give me those feathers!" he bellowed.

"Bart!" Cal Tanner's voice was soft, but there was a threat in it that stopped Bart Clements short.

"You've been deviling that boy past endurance the whole trip," Cal said softly. "I've got a bellyful of it, and so have the others. Dave keeps his feathers. I'm warning you, Bart, don't lay your hand on him, or you'll wish you hadn't!"

Bart glared at him, body tensed. For a moment he seemed about to spring; then slowly his eyes fell before the steely gaze of the redheaded giant. His body relaxed. He gave an uneasy laugh. "I don't want his blamed feathers," he growled, "but he's got to learn who's boss here."

Cal Tanner made no reply, but stood looking at him. Bart turned with an ugly laugh and strode away.

David stepped up to Cal, looking up at him with shining eyes. "Much obliged, Cal! You did me a favor I won't ever forget!"

The giant clapped him gently on the shoulder. "You let me know any time Bart's kicking you around," he said, and walked away.

Buffalo Stampede

4

Amos gave David a hunk of sowbelly and a cold biscuit, then squatted down and examined the eagle feathers by the light of the fire.

"You done it, Dave," he said gleefully. "If you can keep these feathers out of Bart's hands, you've good as got yourself a buffalo runner. A first-class one, too, for you had luck. You got black-tipped feathers."

"Aren't all of them black tipped?"

Amos shook his head. "Not by no long sight. These be as pretty as any I ever seen."

"Amos, what did Cal mean, saying they had more important things to worry about?"

Amos's face darkened. "Injuns again," he said shortly. "Him and Bart and Roy come across their trail not five miles west of here. Twenty or thirty in the party, and their tracks just a few hours old."

"You reckon we got the cavvy hobbled good and strong?"

"They're all right. Bart's posting guard early tonight. Me and you drawed the midnight watch. Best turn in, Dave. You won't get much chance to sleep after our watch. Bart's decided to push on, come sunup. He plain don't like that Injun sign."

The wagon train moved out at dawn. The sun came up blazing hot in a cloudless sky. Hour after hour they crept across the plain. The trail wound in and around arroyos that cut deep into the sun-scorched prairie. Wagon wheels rattled. Drivers geed and hawed at their oxen, forcing them on with cracking bullwhips. Nervous tension had gripped the emigrants. Report had it that the Sioux and the Pawnees were letting the wagon trains pretty much alone, but even the greenhorns in the party knew that no horses were safe from marauding bands of Indians.

They reached Horse Creek at dusk. They forded the creek and camped on the bank. Bart doubled the sentinels and posted double guards to ride herd on the stock.

The next day was a repetition of the day before. Dust billowed up from the wagon wheels, half suffocating those unfortunate enough to have end positions in the line. By afternoon David and Amos were speaking in hoarse croaks. Their eyes were bloodshot. When they moved dust rose in puffs from their clothes.

They camped early, a hundred yards back from a bluff overlooking the Platte. There was no grass. Bart ordered all stock driven down a narrow rocky trail to the stretch of pasture between bluff and river.

Amos and David drew the first shift to ride night herd. They both felt fresher, for they had bathed in the river before supper. At the bottom of the bluff they split up, circling the grazing herd from opposite directions.

From time to time Amos's hoarse bellow would roll through the darkness: "All's well?"

And David would answer: "All's well."

The boy turned the collar of his jacket up around his ears. The night wind blew cold. He glanced up at the stars, big and bright in the blackness of the sky. In the east the moon rose big and full. From high on the hills beyond the river a wolf howled lonesomely, then another, and another. The boy shivered.

Cal Tanner and Roy Edwards relieved them at ten o'clock. Amos and David hobbled their mounts, then lugged saddles and rifles up the bluff and across to the circle of wagons. They were asleep the moment they hit their bedrolls.

Bart Clements shook them awake before dawn.

"Injuns?" Amos barked, snatching up his rifle.

"Wagon trouble," Bart growled. Couple spokes out of a wheel on the little supply wagon. Get them fixed, and then bring up the cavvy."

Amos crawled out. "Make a pot of coffee, Dave, while I get started on that wheel."

Night was fading into the gray of dawn when David carried coffeepot and mugs across the circle. Campfires were crackling. Men and women bustled about in the shadows. From the wagons came the whimpers of sleepy children.

David found Amos sitting under the supply wagon, trying to hammer a spoke into socket.

The old man reached for a mug, took a quick swig, and set it on the ground.

David squatted down beside him, nursing his hot mug between his palms. "Can I help, Amos?"

"Grab hold of this spoke with both hands, Dave, and hold her steady."

Amos slid down on his back. He shifted the spoke a quarter of an inch and raised the hammer. Suddenly he froze. His face paled. Slowly he lowered the hammer.

"What's wrong, Amos? Amos! What's the matter?"

"Shh!" The old man rolled over and pressed his ear to the ground, mouth open, breath whistling. Suddenly he rolled out from under the wagon and leaped to his feet. "Buffalo!" he bellowed. "Buffalo!"

He tore out at a run across the circle, yelling at the top of his lungs. "Buffalo! Buffalo stampede! They're headed straight for us!"

The camp was thrown into pandemonium. Men snatched up their rifles, shouting to their women to take to the wagons. Children screamed. Bart Clements was there, buckling on his pistols, a black scowl on his face.

"Which way?" he shouted above the uproar.

"Out of the west!" Amos was pouring rifle balls from his pouch into his hat. "Heading straight for us. Dave, hand me my powder horn and patches and caps."

Bart turned and raced to the center of the circle of wagons. "All men under the wagons on the west!" he shouted. "Women and children get out from that side. We ain't got a chance, unless we split them. Get your ammunition on the ground in front of you. Hold your fire till I give the signal!"

As suddenly as it had started, the uproar died. Grim-faced men crouched beneath the wagons, rifles thrust through the spokes of the wheels. David crawled under beside Amos. The old man was staring toward the west.

"Pour your balls and patches and caps in your hat," he ordered, without turning his head.

The boy obeyed. Amos fished a plug of tobacco out of his pocket and bit off a corner, working it into his cheek. David narrowed his eyes, trying to see what Amos saw. At first he could make out nothing. Then, as his eyes grew accustomed to the dim light, he saw what looked like a low flying cloud rolling toward them from the horizon. He choked back a cry.

"Dust," Amos grunted, jaws rotating rhythmically. "Must be a thousand of the varmints."

The cloud rolled nearer and nearer. David wet his lips and settled his rifle firmly against his shoulder. As the dust billowed and lifted, he caught glimpses of massive, plunging brown shapes.

Bart Clements's voice rang out. "Remember, we got to split the herd! Every man aim for a bull at the center of the line. You got to load faster'n you ever done! When I give the signal, go for the ones dead center!"

A steady rumble, like thunder, rolled down from the racing buffalo. Their front was a solid brown line stretching across the prairie.

David's finger twitched nervously on the trigger. His eyes took another quick inventory of powder horn and patches and balls and caps on the ground before him. He glanced up at the thundering buffalo. Through the cloud of dust he saw a solid line of massive brown heads stretched low to the ground.

"Fire!" Bart yelled.

Fifty rifles cracked. The onsweeping line did not waver. David choked back a groan as he rammed a ball home in his rifle barrel. The firing was sporadic now, each man loading and shooting as fast as he could.

The buffalo were not a hundred yards away. The thunder of their hoofs muffled the crack of the guns. Suddenly a buffalo in the center went down, then another, and another. The buffalo behind tumbled and sprawled over their bodies. More fell. The herd began to edge away from both sides of the mass of fallen bodies. Rifles cracked. Another went down. The split widened. On each side buffalo at the center pressed and shoved as they galloped, forcing the others to swerve out.

Men yelled as they shot, but the thunder of hoofs drowned out their voices. The herd was splitting. A wild, tossing brown stream of maddened buffalo plunged by not twenty yards out from both sides of the wagon train.

Suddenly Amos let out a yell. "Injuns!" he hollered. "Injuns are running them!"

At that moment David spotted an Indian on a paint pony racing parallel to, and outside, the stampeding buffalo. As he watched, open-mouthed, he saw the Indian brandish a lance over his head. The next instant the Indian was gone in the cloud of dust.

The emigrants had stopped shooting. They lay wide-eyed, watching the buffalo stream past. David kept his gaze on the outer fringe of the herd. He counted nine Indians riding outside the split.

All at once he jerked upright. "Amos!" he screamed. "Amos, look! There's a Injun boy riding inside the buffalo. He's caught in the stampede. He can't get out."

Amos turned, saw the Indian boy astride a pinto pony racing along inside the galloping stream of buffalo. For a moment the boy's face turned toward them. Then boy and pinto suddenly vanished.

"Arroyo!" Amos shouted to David. "Those crazy buffalo took him off into a arroyo. Another dead Injun."

David gazed dazedly at the plunging shaggy brown backs that flowed over the spot. He felt sick. To be caught in the middle of a stampede of maddened buffalo and ridden down. He shuddered.

"Maybe the buffalo will jump over him. Maybe they won't trample him," he almost begged Amos.

The old man spat deliberately. "Not a chance."

"Look!" David screamed. "There's his pony running with the herd. They didn't get the pony."

"Well, you can bet your life they got the Injun," Amos grunted. "Come on, Dave, let's take a look at the carcasses. Those few stragglers won't harm us."

Little Bear

5

David followed Amos toward the piled-up carcasses. He paused when they reached the body of an old bull sprawled forward on its front legs, massive head outstretched. The boy squatted down and peered wonderingly into the small eyes, glazed by death. He reached out and touched the shaggy black fur on the big head.

Bart stopped beside the boy. He kicked the old bull contemptuously. "Mangy old varmint," he spat. "Look at that scabby hide. No good for nothing. Meat'd be rank."

David followed him over to the pile of shaggy giants.

"Twelve," Amos announced to the wagon boss, "but just two cows fit to eat."

"Might as well butcher," Bart decided. "Roy, you fetch a long chain and a yoke of oxen. We'll have to pull this pile apart to get at the cows. Cal, you pick a couple men to ride sentinel. I don't figure those Sioux will be back, but we can't take chances."

"Bart," David spoke up eagerly, "Amos and I saw the buffalo run an Injun boy down over there in an arroyo. His pony got away, but the boy's still there. All right if I go over and see how bad he's hurt?"

"You lost your wits?" Bart roared. "Help an Injun!"

"But he wasn't any bigger than me," David persisted. "We can't just leave him lying there, maybe hurt bad."

"Why can't we? Listen, you blockhead, Injuns be our mortal enemy, man or boy. You think they wouldn't leave you lying there if it was you hurt? If they were merciful, they'd fill you full of arrows. You'd be lucky if they did."

Amos took one look at David's mutinous face and backed Bart up. "Bart's right, Dave. You might as well learn now that the only good Injun is a dead Injun."

David turned away, choking back the indignation that burned in him. He gazed toward the arroyo, clenching his fists at the thought of the boy lying there alone.

"Dave," Bart snarled. "Wake up. Fetch my skinning knife from my gear. Get a move on."

The boy obeyed numbly. He returned with the knife, then stood by, fetching and carrying while the men skinned and butchered the cows. He said nothing more about the Indian boy, but kept glancing furtively toward the arroyo, watching for sign of life.

Cal Tanner sensed his suffering. He paused as he walked past and clapped the boy on the shoulder. "This is one time Bart's right, Dave," he murmured. "Don't worry. If the boy's alive, the Injuns will pick him up soon as we're gone."

"He may be dead by then," the boy muttered, breaking away from the kind hand and stumbling blindly toward the rear of the wagon train.

Amos found him crouched by their fire when he fetched back a buffalo tongue after the butchering. "Got us a prize on account of I gave the warning," he chortled, holding up the long black tongue.

David refused to look up.

"It'll make prime eating, boy. You won't find nothing tastier on the whole prairie."

"I'm not hungry," the boy muttered.

The old man peered at him with wise old eyes. "Still fretting about that Injun boy, ain't you?"

"It's not right," David said stubbornly. "It wouldn't have hurt Bart to let me just go and see if I could help."

"Come on, Dave," Amos switched subjects gently, "we got to get the cavvy up. Most of the wagons are ready to pull out. Even got that supply wagon wheel fixed while they were butchering."

All the while they were driving up the cavvy from the river, David nursed his grievance. Amos said nothing more, but studied the boy out of the corner of his eye. The wagons were creaking into position in the line. Far up at the head they could see Bart sitting on his big bay. Amos and David herded the cavvy in behind the last wagon and reined up, waiting.

[43]

At last the signal came, carried back from wagon to wagon on the loud singsong of the drivers. "Let 'er roll! Let 'er roll!"

One after another the wagons lurched into motion. Dust billowed up from under their wheels. Oxen strained against their yokes as they began the long steep climb toward the high ridge ahead.

Amos and David turned their faces away from the dust. David gazed bleakly toward the arroyo. Amos watched him, pulling at his beard undecidedly. All at once he spoke.

"Your eyes are better'n mine, Dave. Can you see where Bart is?"

David craned his neck, squinting through the dust. "He's already out of sight over the ridge. The lead wagons are over, too."

Amos took off his battered old hat and ran calloused fingers through his grizzled hair. He cleared his throat noisily. "If a fellow herding cavvy were to wait till the last wagon got over that ridge," he said casually, "don't reckon nobody in the wagons could see him, were he to high-tail it back down and look for that Injun boy."

David looked at him, blue eyes shining. "But what about the cavvy?" he stammered.

"I reckon I can manage that long," Amos said

dryly. "Ho, time for us to move out, Dave. Haw, there, you dad-blasted ox! Get going!"

They started the cavvy up the steep slope, taking their time, letting the wagons get ahead. When the last canvas top jounced over the ridge and vanished, Amos turned to the boy. "Now," he said sharply. "And, Dave, look to it you get back before Bart's liable to call a halt. Be no way I could cover up for you then."

David wheeled his mule around. "Much obliged, Amos. I'll hurry." He dug his heels into the mule and raced back down the slope.

At the bottom he reined up, peering through the pall of dust still clinging to the ground. There toward the left was the arroyo. He kicked the mule into a gallop across the rutted plain. On the brink of the arroyo he reined up and sat gazing down into the narrow cut. The bottom was trampled by buffalo hoofs. There was no sign of the Indian boy.

David put the mule down the crumbling bank. The sandy floor stretched empty as far as he could see. He hesitated, glancing up and down. Suddenly his eyes caught a fleck of scarlet fifty feet down to the left. He swung the mule toward it, searching the banks for some sign of the Indian.

As he drew close, David's heart began to hammer. The scarlet was the dyed feather of an arrow that stuck up at an angle from a spotted leopard quiver. A little beyond lay a broken bone bow.

David sent the mule forward at a walk. He scanned the banks. Ahead lay a sharp bend. As the mule eased around, he snorted in terror and reared. David fought him down, holding him with a tight rein. On the ground lay the Indian boy, sprawled face up, eyes closed, hands out-flung.

For a moment David sat still, studying the motionless figure. The boy was smaller than he, and stockier. He wore only breechclout and moccasins. His skin was like smooth copper. His hair was in two long braids.

David tucked his rifle under his arm and swung down, dropping the reins to the ground. Step by step he crept toward the still figure. Suddenly his eyes caught the uneven rise and fall of the boy's chest. He was alive.

David propped his rifle against the bank and knelt down. Blood from a cut over one eye had dried on the boy's cheek. Chest and abdomen and legs had ugly bruises. David choked back an exclamation when he saw the right ankle. It was swollen and discolored. The moccasin cut in tightly through the puffy flesh.

With gentle fingers David probed the swelling. There were no broken bones. He pulled his knife from his belt and cut away the moccasin. Blood had seeped under the toenails, turning them purple. Thin scarlet threads of broken blood vessels showed through the swollen flesh.

David turned back and studied the still copper face. He jerked off his kerchief and wet it from his water flask. Gently he sponged the grime and blood away.

He was almost finished when he caught the slight flutter of the boy's eyelids. David bent over him. Slowly the boy's eyes opened and he looked up blankly into David's face. David smiled and held the flask to his lips. "Drink," he said softly.

The boy took a few quick swallows, staring wide-eyed at the white boy.

"Don't be afraid," David told him. "I'm your friend. You understand? Friend."

"No kill?" the Indian boy whispered.

"No, no kill," David said. "I want to help you."

"Help?"

"Say, you talk English good."

"Learn at Fort Laramie," the boy murmured.

"That's where I'm headed," David told him,

[47]

"but I stayed back behind the wagons to help you."

The boy smiled shyly. "My father make you good present. Me, Little Bear. My father, Chief Strong Wind."

"My name's David."

"Daveed. Your father chief of your village?"

"My father's dead," David said gruffly. "My mother, too."

Little Bear touched his arm softly, making a low murmuring sound.

David got up briskly. "Little Bear, your foot's hurt bad. You think you can get up if I help?"

Little Bear struggled to his feet, clinging to David's arm, but when he put his weight on the injured foot, beads of sweat appeared on his forehead.

"We've got to get you on the mule," David told him. "Hang onto that bush there till I fetch him."

He led the mule up beside Little Bear. "Grab hold of the saddle with both hands," he told him. "Good. When I squat down, you put your good foot in my hands. Then I can lift you up. Understand? Here goes, then."

He got the moccasined foot into his cupped hands. Slowly he straightened up, heaving Little Bear onto the mule. "Get astraddle behind the saddle," he told him.

Little Bear squirmed around until he got his injured leg over the mule's back. Then he sat up with a weak grin. "Do," he said proudly.

"So far, so good." David picked up his rifle and climbed into the saddle. "Which way your camp?"

"Camp?" Little Bear asked puzzledly.

"Your camp—your tepee. Which way?"

Little Bear pointed to the east. "Not far."

"Good," David grunted, and put the mule up the bank of the arroyo. "Hang on, Little Bear. We don't want you falling off now."

David held the mule to a fast walk as they started out across the prairie. "You want me to hold your leg up over mine?" he asked. "Might not hurt so much, that way."

"Not bad," Little Bear refused.

The sun burned down upon them. Dust puffed out from under the hoofs of the mule. Sagebrush and cactus were coated with the fine white sand that the wind lifted and scattered. David took off his hat and wiped his brow.

"Hot," he grunted.

"The Great Spirit smiles," Little Bear agreed placidly. "Where you journey, Daveed?"

"I've got a job herding cavvy—that's driving the loose stock—on a wagon train traveling to Oregon."

[49]

"You set your tepee up there," Little Bear nodded.

"No, I'm going back home to Missouri. I signed up for the round trip."

"Uh?"

David tried again. "My tepee lies many days' journey to the east," he began, pointing. "I live with the mother and the brother of my father."

Little Bear grunted.

"The brother of my father is gone on warpath many moons," David continued, grinning at the thought of his Uncle Andrew down on the Arkansas with General Gaines. "I journey west to provide food for the mother of my father."

"The old mother, she the chief of your village," Little Bear nodded sagely.

"She the chief," David chuckled. In his mind he could see his grandma calmly picking a wild turkey out of a tree with the long rifle. "She heap big chief."

"Daveed," Little Bear interposed, "we go the big rocks there."

David swung the mule toward a dry draw between two eroded sandstone boulders, put him up a sandy, crumbling bank, then sent him up the steep cactus covered slope that climbed toward a high ridge.

"Tepee other side ridge," Little Bear told him.

The mule snorted and wheezed up the slope. They reached the top. David reined up, a low exclamation escaping him, and sat staring with shining eyes.

In a narrow green valley below a double row of yellow tepees stood in a huge circle on the bank of a wide stream. Cooking fires crackled under swinging black pots. Women and children scurried in and out among the tepees. Dogs barked. Horses whinnied. In the shade of the big cotton woods on the bank of the stream stood a line of ponies hitched to empty travois.

"What are they doing?" David asked. "Where are they going?"

"Follow hunters to prairie," Little Bear told him. "Many buffalo killed. Women skin. Bring meat and robes back on travois."

David sat staring silently down at the camp.

"We go," Little Bear said, tugging at his sleeve. "My mother cook us buffalo meat, and—" he broke off, cocking his head to one side.

"What's the matter? What do you hear?"

"Ponies follow us." Little Bear twisted around. "It is my father!" he cried joyfully. "And Standing Wolf and Star Watcher. They have brought back Fleet Deer, my buffalo runner."

David swung the mule around, his heart hammering. Twenty feet behind them three Indian men sat stolidly on paint ponies, regarding him with expressionless faces. Sunlight glinted on naked copper bodies. The wind lifted the eagle feathers in their long black hair. One brave sat a little in front of the other two. In his hand he held the braided rein of a riderless pinto pony.

David licked dry lips. The brave in front—the one leading the pony—must be Strong Wind, Little Bear's father, chief of the village.

Trouble at Fort Laramie

6

Little Bear broke into a torrent of Sioux. David caught the sound of his name. He knew that Little Bear was telling his father about the accident and David's finding him.

Before the expressionless stares of the Indian braves David for the first time knew fear. The echo of Bart's warning sounded in his ears. He shivered. Cold sweat broke out over his body. Behind him Little Bear's voice droned on and on, but now David imagined there was a sinister quality to it.

Suddenly Little Bear broke off. Strong Wind touched his pony forward until he was beside the mule. Inscrutable black eyes scanned the cut on his son's forehead, traveled down over the scratched dirty body, rested broodingly on the swollen discolored foot.

David wet his lips nervously. He stared furtively at the strong copper face so near his own, noting the proud arched nose, the thin unsmiling lips.

Suddenly the chief spoke, his voice deep and guttural. "Standing Wolf find Little Bear's pony running in buffalo herd," he said flatly. "Strong Wind ride back to look for son. See where Little Bear fall. See tracks of mule. See tracks of white boy's boots. Think Little Bear taken wagon train."

He stopped. David thought for a moment that he saw suffering in the hard black eyes. Then the chief continued. "Strong Wind follow tracks. See tracks go toward village. No understand."

David cleared his throat nervously. Strong Wind looked hard at him. "You come wagon train?" he asked.

David nodded. "Wagon train," he echoed huskily.

"Why you ride back?"

"See buffalo run Little Bear down," David stammered. "Him hurt. Me help."

"Why white boy help Indian boy?"

David forgot his fear for the moment. "Him person," he began hesitantly, searching for words the chief could understand. "Him boy. Me boy. Me help."

Strong Wind pondered this. "Wagon chief know white boy ride back?" he asked at last.

David flushed. "No."

Strong Wind shook his head. "White boy heap brave to leave wagon train. Now wagon train gone. What you do?"

"Ride fast. Catch up."

Again the chief shook his head. "White boy fool. White boy got thunderstick. Him alone on prairie. Pawnees scout buffalo close to running water. Pawnees catch white boy. Kill him for thunderstick."

David glanced down at his rifle balanced across his knees. He shivered. Strong Wind was serious about the Pawnees.

One of the braves called to the chief in Sioux. Strong Wind listened intently, then turned back to David.

"Standing Wolf say better white boy stay in Indian village this night. Wagon train stop Fort

Laramie. When sun rise he take white boy to fort."

"I'm much obliged, Chief Strong Wind," David said earnestly, "but I've got to go to wagon train now. Wagon chief heap mad if he know white boy help Injun boy."

Strong Wind swung his pony around and rode over to the two braves. They conferred, heads close together. David waited nervously. From time to time one of the braves would turn and look at him, then return to the discussion. Finally Strong Wind rode back over to the boys.

"Little Bear only son in Strong Wind's tepee," he said slowly. "White boy risk life to help Little Bear. Strong Wind not forget. Strong Wind white boy's friend."

"I'm much obliged, Chief Strong Wind."

"You go wagon train now. Standing Wolf and Star Watcher ride with white boy. No harm come."

"Daveed no go!" Little Bear protested. "Go to tepee. Be Little Bear's brother."

Strong Wind swung to the ground, nodding for the braves to come help. Guarding the injured foot tenderly, they lifted the protesting Little Bear off the mule and seated him astride his own pony.

"Daveed, no go," Little Bear pleaded.

"I've got to go, Little Bear," David said earnestly. "Wagon train stop Fort Laramie three, four days. Maybe I can see you."

Strong Wind swung to his pony's back. "White boy make good medicine for Little Bear. White boy always welcome in tepee of Strong Wind. Go in peace."

The two Indian braves set a stiff pace across the prairie on their stout little ponies. They followed no trail. David gave the mule his head and hung on, hoping grimly that the mule would keep out of the prairie-dog holes that dotted the plain.

Mile ofter mile fell behind them. Standing Wolf and Star Watcher seemed determined to deliver David to the wagon train in as short a time as possible. The boy was grateful. He could tell from the sun that the day was past noon. He felt a sick heaviness in his stomach. Bart would know by now what he had done. Amos would not have been able to hide his absence at the nooning halt.

Up and down over the barren slopes they raced, slowing when ponies and mule lagged tiredly, stopping on top of high ridges and scanning the prairie for enemy sign.

On the far side of one high ridge they rode out suddenly onto the rutted tracks of the trail. Standing Wolf, who was in the lead, swung his pony parallel to the deep ruts. They followed them down and across a sun-scorched plain, angling slowly toward a line of big cottonwoods that marked the banks of the Platte.

All at once David spied a rough log fort nestled beneath the trees. It was not Fort Laramie, for Amos had told him of the high walls of adobe brick there.

"Mr. Standing Wolf," David called. "Mr. Star Watcher."

Without slowing their ponies they looked back.

David pointed toward the log structure. "What fort?"

"Fort of white trader," Star Watcher called.

They were close to the fort now. David could see two Indian lodges pitched close beside the building. As they drew abreast a dozen naked Indian children popped out of the lodges, trailed by a pack of mongrel dogs. The children watched stolidly as the riders galloped past. The dogs raced alongside, barking furiously, then gradually dropping back. David twisted in his saddle, watching the fort until he could see it no longer.

For the next hour they followed the course of the Platte across the plain. Ahead loomed a chain of barren hills. The prairie began to give way to rough slopes.

They came at last to a steep hill. Ponies and

mule slogged up through caving sand. Standing Wolf reached the top first. "Fort Laramie!" he called back.

David urged the mule up. They reached the top. The boy sat staring.

At the bottom of the ridge the plain reached out for a quarter of a mile to where a narrow river churned and tumbled down to meet the wide, swift-flowing Platte. Beyond the junction of the rivers the long rectangular fort with its two tall blockhouses and its pale adobe walls towered high above the prairie that stretched away toward the blue rim of distant mountains.

Clusters of Indian tepees dotted the plain before the fort. Well off to one side were the white circles of wagon-train encampments.

Standing Wolf gazed stolidly at the stream roaring down between them and the fort. "River flood. Bad medicine for wagon train."

He led out down the rutted trail toward the muddy, swollen river. All along the trail down to the bank were heavy household possessions discarded to lighten wagon loads. David recognized the Edwards' brand new iron cook stove and a little later spied Cal Tanner's good walnut bedstead.

They passed carved chests and stout rocking chairs, more stoves, and a heavy oak table. The river bank was littered with pots and furniture.

They reined up at the ford. David gazed uneasily at the surging water, staring with misgiving at the big tree trunks hurtling downstream.

"Me go first," Standing Wolf announced. "White boy follow. Star Watcher come last. White boy give mule his head. Hang onto saddle."

David obeyed. The mule followed Standing Wolf's pony out into the rushing current. Water foamed up around his knees, covered David's feet, then boiled up around the saddle. David held his rifle high with one hand and hung onto the pommel with the other. The mule was swimming. The boy gazed fearfully at a tree trunk that the angry flood was bearing down toward them. Suddenly he felt the mule find footing. They went scrambling and slipping up the muddy bank. Ponies and mule were heaving by the time they reached the top.

"Stop, get wind," Standing Wolf grunted.

Suddenly he bent sideways from his pony and studied the welter of tracks in the mud. He said something to Star Watcher, and they swung their ponies down along the bank at a walk. David followed curiously.

Thirty feet down the Indians uttered low exclamations and reined up, gazing down into the tall grass. David crowded the mule up close. His eyes got big.

"It's the wagon boss's roan mare!" he cried.

The mare lay on her side. Her eyes were glazed by death. A jagged hole ran the length of her belly.

"Tree got her," Standing Wolf grunted. "She swim out. Die here."

David felt sick. "Bart aimed to make a buffalo runner out of her," he said dully. "Bart thought a heap of that mare."

Star Watcher looked at him gravely. "White boy troubled."

"You wouldn't understand," David said miserably. "I was supposed to be herding cavvy. Wagon boss blame me."

Standing Wolf shot the boy a keen glance. "We go now. White boy ride to fort alone. Bad medicine if white man see white boy with Indians."

David tried to smile. "Dead mare already make bad medicine," he said ruefully. "I'm much obliged to you both for guiding me here."

"Strong Wind say see white boy safe," Standing Wolf told him. "We go Fort Laramie. You no see Standing Wolf and Star Watcher. We see white boy."

David waved good-by and turned the mule toward the fort. In the distance he could see Indians and emigrants scurrying in and out the wide-open gates.

The boy swung the mule right, toward the wagon encampments. A hundred feet from the first circle of wagons he reined up, heart pounding. It was his wagon train. There was the cavvy, staked and grazing beyond the circle.

The boy touched the mule forward. He was within twenty feet of the wagons when all at once three men stepped out from between two wagons and started down to meet him. David began to sweat. It was Amos and Cal and Bart Clements.

They met. David reined the mule to a halt. One quick glance at Amos's and Cal's unhappy faces was enough. The boy looked fearfully at Bart. The wagon boss's face was set and hard. His black eyes bored into David's. His one outward sign of fury was the slow clenching and unclenching of big hairy fists.

"Get down!" he said in a strained flat voice.

David obeyed numbly. He waited beside the mule, his heart hammering.

"You sneaking double-crosser!" Bart snarled. "So you came back! I figured I was rid of you. Why didn't you stay with your Injun friends, if you love them so much?"

David began to tremble. Never had he seen such hate as in Bart Clements's face.

"Reckon you'll get down on your knees and beg me to forgive you, next," Bart sneered. "Wasn't for these mealymouthed friends of yours here, I'd give you a quirting that'd have you bellowing for mercy!"

David licked his lips nervously. He pressed shaking hands against his thighs.

"You yellow-bellied snake!" Bart screamed suddenly. "I'm going to learn you a lesson you'll remember! You're walking cavvy two weeks for stealing my mule!"

"But I didn't steal your mule," David protested.

"Shut up and listen to me!" Bart shouted. "That was just the beginning. You're losing three months' wages for deserting your post."

"Three months!" David stammered. "That's not fair!"

Bart's face went livid. He took a quick step forward and hit the boy a brutal blow across the face with the back of his fist, slamming him to the ground. "Talk back to me, will you!" he screamed, drawing back his foot and aiming a savage kick at the boy sprawled on the ground.

Cal Tanner leaped forward, grabbed Bart, and spun him around. "That's enough, Bart!" he said heavily. "You've done it. I hope you feel better for it!"

"Let me go!" Bart screamed, struggling to get free. "He didn't care what happened to my mare! Let him crawl back to his Injun friends!"

"Enough's enough, Bart," Cal told him. "The boy made a mistake. You've punished him. Now forget it."

David struggled up on one elbow, swiping at the flow of blood from his nose with his sleeve. Amos jerked off his kerchief and knelt to help the boy.

"Dave couldn't have saved the mare," he said reasonably. "We was all there, and we couldn't do it."

Bart jerked free of Cal's grasp and turned toward the wagons. "Just you two keep that Duncan whelp out of my reach!" he snarled. "I'm warning you. Keep him out of my reach!"

When he was gone Amos and Cal helped David to his feet.

"What am I going to do now?" the boy hiccupped, staunching his nosebleed with Amos's kerchief.

"Stick to your job and stop traipsing around playing the Good Samaritan," Cal advised. "Wait till Bart cools off. I'll have a talk with him. I think I can get him to go a bit easier on you then."

"Cal's right, Dave," Amos nodded. "Bart'll simmer down. We'll talk him around, don't you worry. You ate anything today, boy?"

"I'm not hungry," David said miserably.

"Once you get a whiff of that buffalo tongue I'm cooking, you will be. We waited for you, Dave."

"Don't you want to hear about the Injun boy? I found him. His name's Little Bear—"

"You tell us while we're eating," Amos said kindly. "Sure hope that blamed Injun was worth this here trouble."

"Let me unsaddle the mule and stake him out first," David told him. "I'll be right on up."

All the time he was unsaddling the mule and staking him out, David cast furtive glances toward the brushy plain that sloped down to the river. Nowhere could he see a sign of Standing Wolf or Star Watcher. Gingerly the boy felt of his face. It was swelling badly. Dully he wondered if Standing Wolf and Star Watcher had seen Bart knock him down.

Blue Thunder

7

David crawled stiffly out of his bedroll at dawn. Gingerly he felt of his swollen face. "My nose feels big as a house," he told Amos.

The old man glanced up from the fire. "Come here, and let me have a look at you. Jumping Jehoshophat! You're a mess! I ain't saw a black eye like that in a month of Sundays!"

David squatted down beside the fire. "I didn't say much last night, Amos, as long as Cal was here, but I've been lying awake half the night, thinking."

"About pulling out from Bart and the train," Amos guessed shrewdly.

David nodded. "It's like this, Amos. I was reading the other day in the Testament Grandma gave me how a fellow ought to turn his other cheek. I don't think that would work with Bart. You know Bart well as I do. Yesterday was just the beginning. I reckon I did wrong, sneaking off to help Little Bear. Trouble is, from now on, everything I do'll be wrong, far as Bart's concerned."

"Maybe it won't be all that bad, Dave."

"Yes it will, and you know it. Grandma warned me not to sign up with Bart. There's been bad feeling between him and Uncle Andrew ever since Uncle Andrew beat him up for robbing his traps when they were just boys."

"So that's what it was," Amos said slowly.

"Me, I wouldn't listen to Grandma. I was bound to come west and try my luck. Fine mess I've made."

"Well, you sure don't look like much at this minute," Amos admitted cheerfully. "Maybe a cup of coffee'll perk you up a mite. Here."

After they had eaten, David helped Amos take off the faulty wheel from the supply wagon. They started out across the prairie toward the fort, David rolling the wheel. The boy stared avidly at the expanse of Indian tepees pitched on the plain before the adobe walls.

"Where'd they all come from!" he asked Amos. "What are so many doing here?"

"They've brought in pelts and buffalo robes and moccasins and such to trade," Amos told him.

"How long will they stay?"

"Long as they got something to trade for fire water, most of them," Amos said dryly. "Poor varmints, they work like dogs all year, and guzzle it down in a couple days."

They were approaching the wide gates. Tall Indian men, wrapped in white buffalo robes, squaws in buckskin dresses embroidered with dyed porcupine quills, emigrants in coarse home-spun and calico, swarmed in and out.

David forgot his swollen face. He gazed spellbound at the scene before them. Atop the high adobe walls bearded men in buckskin stood in little groups, talking and laughing as they watched the stream of people. Blockhouses crowned two opposite corners of the wall. Directly over the gate was a tall blockhouse, with two shiny brass cannons pointed toward the prairie. Beyond was the long roof of the main building.

Amos and David pushed through the crowd at the gate. They found themselves in a huge courtyard. To one side an adobe wall fenced off a long narrow corral. Shops and apartments and offices lined the other sides.

"Now, lessee," Amos muttered, "the smithy's down this way, well as I recollect."

David rolled the clumsy wheel in and out through the milling crowd, keeping close to the old man's heels. He passed a group of bearded buckskin-clad men. The butts of their long rifles rested on the ground. The men were laughing and talking as they passed a jug from hand to hand. Trappers down from the mountains, the boy guessed excitedly.

The smithy was an open shed against the wall. David gaped unashamedly at the smith. The man towered over Amos. Naked to the waist, he wore buckskin pants and leather apron. Arms and chest and belly were pelted with curly black hair.

"You'll have to leave the wheel," the smith growled to Amos. "I'll have it fixed by tomorrow. That'll give you plenty time to have yourself a fling."

"Reckon it'll give me more'n enough," Amos told him. "Mind you do a good job. Bart Clements ain't the man to take poor work lying down."

"Bart Clements," the smith growled. "I already seen Bart. He's met up with some pals of his, mountain men from the Rockies. This time tomorrow, Bart won't know a wheel from a wagon tongue."

Amos nodded to David, and they left. The old man led the way across to the store. While he dickered for flour and tobacco, David stood at the door and watched the crowd.

Amos joined him there. "We best get on back to the camp," he told the boy. "We got our work cut out for us there. Money's all gone, anyways. Flour a dollar a pound!"

They kept busy at odd jobs the rest of the day. They saw nothing of Bart. Cal Tanner stopped by for a moment in the afternoon.

"Bart's sleeping it off up at the fort," he scowled. "Those mountain pals of his drunk him under the table."

Amos shook his head. "Bart'll be like a sore-headed bear for a week," he growled. "Blame fool! He'll need a clear head from here on into Oregon."

They crawled into their bedrolls at dark, bone weary. David lay awake, staring up at the starry sky. From the fort drifted the faint music of an accordian. Somebody was playing "My Old Kentucky Home." A sudden wave of homesickness welled up in the boy. In the dark he fumbled in his pouch until his fingers found the little Testament. Back home Grandma would have gone to bed, too. Likely it was lonely for her in the cabin. Tears stung the boy's eyes. He buried his face in his old blanket and cried himself to sleep.

Next morning Amos set out for the fort after breakfast. David stayed behind to grease the axles on the rest of the supply wagons. He was hard at work toward the middle of the morning when Roy Edwards's oldest boy, Sammy, came running down across the prairie from the fort.

"David!" the youngster hollered. "David!"

David stuck his head out from behind the wagon. "Here, Sammy. What'd you want?"

The boy pulled up, panting excitedly. "Pa says you're to come up to the fort," he gasped, eyes big and round. "There's a Injun Chief looking for you, David. A real Injun Chief and two Injun braves! Come on! Hurry!"

David set down the bucket of grease and wiped his hands on the grass. His heart was pounding. It could not be anyone but Strong Wind and Standing Wolf and Star Watcher.

"Let's go!" he told Sammy, and they set out for the fort at a run.

Just inside the big gate David pulled up short. In the middle of a crowd of emigrants and trappers Strong Wind and the two braves were sitting stolidly on their ponies. From the crowd came an excited babble of voices.

"Chief Strong Wind!" David called, but the chief did not hear him over the noise.

Suddenly a man's hoarse bass rang out. "Shut up for a minute, all of you!" he yelled, and the crowd fell silent. "I've made the chief a offer for the horse," the man continued in a normal tone. "I'm making it again and for the last time. One hundred dollars cash money and my bobtail mule. Take it or leave it."

"No take," came Strong Wind's solemn voice.

"Ask him where he stole the horse!" a bearded trapper shouted drunkenly. "That stallion ain't no Injun pony. That's a blooded horse!"

David tried to elbow his way through the crowd. "Chief Strong Wind!" he called again.

This time the chief heard him. All at once the crowd parted, and Strong Wind stalked slowly through toward David.

The boy stared. Strong Wind was leading a big stallion by a plaited jaw rope. The stallion was a pale silver gray, with long flowing black mane and tail. He stepped proudly on long powerful legs, tossing his head until the black mane flew.

"Hello, Chief Strong Wind," David said shyly. "That's a beautiful stallion. What's his name?"

"His name Blue Thunder," Strong Wind grunted. "Him buffalo runner."

David stepped softly over to the stallion and stroked the arched gray neck. "I'm glad to see you. How's Little Bear?"

"Medicine man make good medicine for sick foot. Little Bear better soon."

"Good."

Strong Wind gazed at the boy's swollen face. "Wagon chief make bad medicine, white boy?" he asked softly.

David tried to grin. "Heap bad."

The crowd was listening curiously. Strong Wind turned his back to them. "Standing Wolf and Star Watcher tell Strong Wind that wagon chief hit white boy. Strong Wind sorry. Come make white boy present. Here!" And he thrust the stallion's rein into David's hand.

David looked incredulously from the rope to the chief's face. "You're giving the stallion to me?" he gasped.

Strong Wind nodded. "Make good present, huh?"

"I—I can't ever thank you enough!" David

gasped. "He's the most beautiful—I—I don't know what to say!"

Strong Wind understood. He touched David's shoulder with gentle fingers. "Me friend white boy," he told him.

After Strong Wind and the two braves had departed, David led Blue Thunder through the curious crowd and out the gate. Sammy Edwards caught up with him outside.

"The chief really gave him to you!" he panted. "Wait till Bart hears! Won't he be mad! Why don't you ride him?"

David was already worrying about Bart. "I don't want to ride yet," he told Sammy absently. "Reckon I'm scared if I do, I'll wake up and find it's a dream."

David staked Blue Thunder on the fringe of the cavvy. Half a dozen men drifted down from the wagons. The dazed boy scarcely heard their admiring exclamations. In the distance he could see Amos hurrying down from the fort. He licked his lips nervously.

Amos came straight to him. "So they're telling the truth up at the fort," he panted. "The chief really gave you a stallion. And by golly, ain't he a beauty!"

"What did Bart say?" David asked anxiously.

The old man's face sobered. "You ain't going to like it, Dave."

"He said I couldn't keep Blue Thunder," David guessed angrily.

"Worse than that, boy. Bart, he aims to claim the horse for his."

"He can't!" David cried mutinously. "Blue Thunder's mine. Strong Wind gave him to me for helping Little Bear."

"On Bart's time and with his mule," Amos reminded him dryly. "I'm scared, Dave. Bart'll find plenty folks to back him up."

"He's not going to take Blue Thunder away from me!" David cried hotly, face white, eyes blazing.

"Bart don't aim to keep the horse, Dave. Trapper fellow's done offered to buy it, and Bart's just about promised. Look! Here comes Bart and the trapper now."

David turned. Bart and a buckskin-clad man were hurrying down across the plain.

"He's not going to sell my horse!" Dave said. "I'll run away first."

"Stop talking foolishness, Dave. No horse is worth all that. Hello, Bart. Come to see the boy's horse?"

Bart Clements ignored the old man. He strode straight across to the gray stallion. Blue Thunder flung his head up and backed nervously away from the wagon boss.

David's heart sank when he saw the trapper. It was the man who had tried to buy Blue Thunder from Strong Wind. The boy started slowly forward, his eyes on the wagon boss. Bart's face was flushed. His eyes were bloodshot. The reek of stale whisky surrounded him.

"I heard I had me a new horse," he said loudly, slurring his words. "I had him figured for just another common Injun pony. Looks like the fellows up to the fort was right. This horse is a half blood at least."

"You're going to stand by your bargain, ain't you, Bart?" the trapper asked anxiously. "You give your word."

David spoke up, heart pounding, body wet with sweat. "Bart's not making any bargains with this horse," he said shakily. "He can't. The horse is mine."

Bart wheeled. With one powerful backward sweep of his fist, he sent the boy tumbling head over heels on the ground. David sprang to his feet, eyes blazing, but Bart was waiting, one big fist drawn back.

"Open your big trap one more time, and you can start walking back to Missouri!" Bart screamed. "I'm boss here, and what I say, goes!

You cost me my roan mare! Now you'll pay for her! You can thank your stars I don't give you the quirting you deserve!"

David gazed at the livid face with loathing.

"You gave your word, Bart!" the trapper repeated anxiously.

Bart gave an ugly laugh. "That was before I saw my new horse, Frank. You think I'd be fool enough to sell this stallion for a hundred dollars?"

"I'll up my offer," the trader growled angrily.

"You're wasting your time," Bart told him. "I ain't selling! Come on back up to the fort, Frank. I'm setting 'em up to celebrate my new horse!"

The trapper followed him sullenly. They had almost reached the wagons when Bart turned back. "Amos," he hollered, "fix that horse up with a real bridle. We're going after buffalo, come morning. I'll see how good a runner he is. And tie a quirt onto the pommel of my saddle. I never seen a Injun horse yet that didn't need beating."

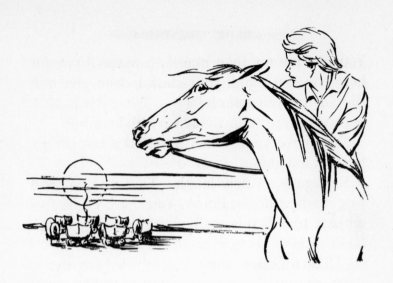

Escape to the Indians

8

From the moment that Bart hit him, David knew that he was going to run away. The boy had a sick feeling. He realized there was no use in his trying any more. Bart was not going to forgive him for leaving the wagon train to help Little Bear.

Now that Strong Wind had given him the

stallion, David did not intend to submit to Bart's mistreatment any longer. "I'll show him," the boy told himself. "I'll find Strong Wind. He'll hide me."

The boy kept turning over in his mind whether to confide in Amos or not. He decided against it.

Noon came. Amos made coffee, and they ate cold tongue and biscuits.

"Bart took the horse away from you," Amos told the boy. "Let him bridle and saddle the critter. I ain't touching him."

David said nothing. As soon as the old man left for the fort after dinner, the boy began his preparations.

He filled his powder horn and packed patches and caps and balls into his bullet pouch. He got his shoulder pouch from the supply wagon and checked to see that the eagle feathers were safe. They would make a fine present for Chief Strong Wind.

He stepped out around the wagon when he was done and squinted down the slope toward the river. He'd have to wait until night and risk fording the river by moonlight. There was no other way to escape without being seen.

He walked down the slope toward the river. Fifty yards from camp he came on a shallow ravine, bushy with sagebrush. The boy went back to the wagon and got rifle and pouches and carried them down and hid them under the shelving bank. Then he went back up to the cavvy and untied Blue Thunder.

The stallion wore a simple Indian braided jaw rope, tied around his lower jaw, the loose end serving as a single rein.

"Guess I can handle you with it," David muttered to the stallion.

He led the stallion around to the far side of the cavvy and restaked him well away from the wagons. The stallion was nervous. He flattened his ears, whinnying shrilly. Carefully the boy set about making friends. With gentle hands he pulled the stallion's head down and breathed into the flaring nostrils, letting the horse get used to his smell. Then he began to stroke the stallion's face and neck, moving slowly around the big horse until he had stroked the entire body. Slowly the stallion relaxed under the boy's hands. When David stopped beside his head again, Blue Thunder gave a soft nicker and nuzzled his cold nose against the boy's face.

David threw both arms about the arched gray neck. "I love you," he said thickly. "Once we get away, it's going to be just you and me together."

At last the boy left the stallion and walked up to the wagons. He felt sick when he thought of leaving without telling Amos good-by. If he could just leave a note, it would be better than nothing. There was a stub of pencil in the supply wagon, but something to write on—suddenly the boy's eyes lighted. Amos's Bible!

David climbed up over the tailgate of the wagon and rummaged out the dog-eared Bible from Amos's sack. Fetching the pencil, he sat down on the tailgate and opened the book to the flyleaf. "Dear Amos," he printed, "I have run away. Don't look for me. I'll be all right. Your friend, David."

That would have to do. He would put the Bible on his bedroll when he left. Amos would find it.

The emigrants began to drift down from the fort toward supper time. Amos came, muttering at the slowness of the blacksmith.

"You all right, Dave?" he asked worriedly.

"I'm all right. The coffee's ready, Amos, and there's plenty of meat left."

The old man looked at him sharply. "You sound mighty cheerful, Dave. I figured on finding you long-faced on account of Bart."

David said nothing, busying himself with the supper. All during the meal Amos studied the boy covertly, a worried frown on his face. As soon as it was dark they spread their bedrolls under the wagon and turned in. Amos tried to talk. David answered in monosyllables. Soon the old man fell asleep. The boy lay quietly in the dark, listening to the rise and fall of Amos's snores.

The full moon rose in the east and climbed in and out behind fleecy clouds that drifted across its face. The camp settled down.

A long time later the sound of men's voices and half-stifled laughter approached from the fort. David recognized Bart's deep voice. Bart had been drinking. He would sleep hard.

Quiet settled over the wagons. The only sound was the muffled steps of the stock as they cropped the grass.

David waited a little longer. A big white cloud was blowing up from the west. He watched until the tip touched the moon, then slipped out of his bedroll. He placed Amos's Bible face down on his blankets, then crept out from under the wagon, and stole around the fringe of the cavvy.

Blue Thunder nickered softly as the boy approached. David spoke to him in a whisper, breathing into the stallion's nostrils, stroking the soft nose. When the horse stood quiet, the boy untied the picket rope and coiled it over his shoulder. Then he grabbed the rein and led the stallion off down the slope to the ravine.

He found his cache without difficulty. Slipping

his rifle strap over his head, he shrugged the rifle easy across his back. Then he slung the pouches over his shoulder and led Blue Thunder down the slope toward the river.

He took his time, glancing back every few yards to make sure he was not followed. The wagons dropped out of sight behind the slope. The river was only a couple of hundred feet away. He could see the silvery ripples gleaming in the moonlight.

Beside a low hummock, David halted the stallion. "Don't make any fuss, Blue Thunder," he whispered, running his hands lightly over the stallion's neck. "I've got to ride you from here on."

Climbing up on the hummock, David eased onto the stallion. Powerful shoulder muscles rippled under the boy's legs. The stallion tensed, ears flattening.

"Easy, boy! Easy! That's my good boy. Easy, now."

Blue Thunder calmed under the boy's voice. He stepped forward quietly under the pressure of David's knees. They approached the river.

"We've got to find the wagon ford," David muttered. "Let's try down this way. Easy, boy! There. There are the ruts. We're all right, now."

He swung the stallion down the trail. Blue Thunder took the bank calmly, bracing his feet

[83]

and sliding down into the current. For twenty feet he splashed through shallow water. Then suddenly the current boiled up against his sides. At that instant David felt him sinking. The stallion floundered wildly.

David panicked. Quicksand! He jerked the picket rope off his shoulder and brought it down with a whack across the gray rump. Blue Thunder lunged in terror, humping his back and floundering free. He hit deep water. He was swimming.

The current swept them a hundred feet below the trail before the stallion found firm footing and scrambled out up the muddy bank beyond the river. David sent him at a canter back up to the trail. The discarded household furnishings from the wagon train loomed ghostly in the moonlight. Blue Thunder shied at a rocking chair that had toppled over onto the rutted tracks. The boy steadied him with voice and knees and swung him away from the river.

The stallion ran effortlessly. The boy felt the smooth rippling of powerful muscles under his knees. The stallion sped up the steep slope of the first hill without slowing. David reined him up at the top and looked back. Across the river the outline of Fort Laramie stood out against the prairie. The boy's eyes located the white gleam of canvas wagon tops in the moonlight. He gazed at them a long moment, throat tightening, tears stinging his eyes.

"Good-by, Amos," he whispered.

The stallion moved restlessly. David swung him back on the trail. "Let's go, Blue Thunder."

Mile after mile fell behind them. The wide silver ribbon of the Platte uncurled on their left. They neared the log fort of the white trader. David circled wide to the south around the fort, so as not to arouse the pack of dogs.

Slowly the sky lightened in the east. Blue Thunder had struck his stride in an easy lope that ate up the miles. David watched the wagon ruts closely. Star Watcher and Standing Wolf had taken him straight across the prairie to Fort Laramie, but the boy knew that the wagon ruts would take him back to the old campsite.

Dawn was coming. The prairie was shimmering in a pinkish glow from the crimson that streaked the eastern sky. David gazed about, trying to spot some familiar landmark.

Blue Thunder sped up a long slope. At the top David reined up, pulse quickening. Below on the prairie lay the circles of blackened campfires where the wagon train had encamped the night before the buffalo stampede. There on the north was the bluff and, below it, the stretch of grass to the river bank.

The boy sent the stallion down past the blackened fire circles to the arroyo where he had found Little Bear. The stallion slid down into the arroyo, swung left under the rein, and followed the cut down to where David had found the Indian boy. David pulled him up and sat studying the sides of the arroyo, biting his lip in concentration.

"Right there's where we climbed out," he said aloud. "There are our tracks, and the tracks of the Indian ponies, too. Up you go, boy."

Back out on the plain, the boy reined up once again. "The sun was in our faces then, just like now," he muttered. "As long as I keep you headed into it, I can't get off far."

He touched the stallion forward. Blue Thunder struck out at a fast walk, heading straight east up and down over sandy sagebrush slopes. David gave him his head.

"Looks to me like you know where you're going," he told the horse. "I'll just let you alone and see."

Suddenly the stallion swung left toward a dry wash. David's heart leaped. Straight ahead, two sandstone boulders jutted up out of the prairie. The boy patted the stallion's neck.

"You did know the way, Blue Thunder! We're almost there!"

The stallion went down into the wash between

the boulders, climbed out beyond, and broke into a lope up the steep slope to the ridge. David's heart was pounding. Just over the ridge lay the Indian village.

They reached the top. David reined up. Blue Thunder whinnied eagerly, prancing under the tight rein. David gazed down into the green valley. Beyond the stream with its borders of cottonwoods lay the great circle of tepees, backed by the brush corral. Thick layers of smoke from open fires eddied over the tepees. Men lounged in the open doors. Women were busy at cooking fires and at drying racks. A bevy of naked boys splashed in the shallow stream. Their carefree shouts mingled with the barking of dogs from the village.

A sudden shyness touched the boy. What would happen if Strong Wind were not in the village? David dreaded riding down alone into the midst of so many strange Indians. He had begun to sweat. He wiped wet palms on his legs.

All at once from close by came the loud snap of a dead branch under a hoof. David jerked around. At that instant an Indian on a shaggy paint pony rode out of a clump of trees on his right.

David started to tremble. The Indian was naked except for breechclout. Three eagle feathers were thrust upright in his hair. Over one shoulder was slung a beaver quiver of arrows. In his hand, he carried a stout wooden bow.

When close, the Indian reined up and raised right hand in the sign of a friend. Then he motioned the frightened boy to follow him.

They started out down the slope to the stream. David could see men jump to their feet before the tepees. Women left their fires. Naked boys ran up out of the stream toward the tepees, pointing excitedly toward David and his escort.

The Indian guard led the way out into the shallow stream. On the opposite bank Indians crowded close. David searched the dark, inscrutable faces anxiously, but nowhere was a familiar face.

The crowd parted to let them through. The guard led the way straight to the largest tepee, close to the center of the village. He reined up and jumped to the ground, ducking into the open entrance.

David sat still. He glanced nervously over his shoulder at the crowd that had followed them. Suddenly an Indian appeared in the entrance of the tepee. It was Chief Strong Wind. He stepped outside, followed by the guard.

David slid to the ground, snatching off his battered hat. "Hello, Chief Strong Wind," he said shyly.

The chief looked down at the boy with searching, yet gentle eyes. "Daveed welcome," he said slowly. "Wagon chief make bad medicine for white boy?"

"He was going to take Blue Thunder away from me!" David burst out. "I've run away!"

"Daveed do good thing," the chief told him. "Blue Thunder belong to Daveed."

At that moment Little Bear came hobbling down between the tepees on a crude wooden crutch.

"Daveed! Daveed!" he cried joyfully. "You've come back!"

White Eagle, My Second Son

9

That afternoon Strong Wind sent out word that all members of the council were bidden to a feast that evening in the tepee of their chief.

Singing Water, Little Bear's pretty mother, bustled about the cooking fire, propping long buffalo ribs on green willow sticks to roast. Pale Fawn and Run Lightly, wives of Standing Wolf and Star Watcher, came to help her. The women were friendly and curious with the white boy. They spoke little, but watched him with bright eyes.

Late in the afternoon Singing Water, at Strong Wind's bidding, brought David a buckskin breechclout and moccasins decorated with dyed porcupine quills and a soft white buffalo robe for his shoulders. Little Bear helped him change in the tepee. The Indian garments felt strange to the white boy. When he followed Little Bear hesitantly out of the tepee, Pale Fawn's black eyes widened at sight of his fair skin. Holding her round coppery arm next to his, she said: "White boy Pale Fawn, not me."

Run Lightly burst into giggles. David blushed. He turned to duck back inside the tepee, but Singing Water caught his arm and held him back. Clucking her tongue reprovingly at the two women, she patted David's shoulder. "New brother of Little Bear has gold hair like Sun Spirit," she said kindly. "Good medicine."

Strong Wind nodded approvingly from his seat beside the tepee entrance. "Good medicine," he echoed, and suddenly David felt better.

The sun sank low in the west. The shadows of the tepees stretched long on the ground. In the tepee of Strong Wind buffalo robes were spread in a circle about the fire in the center.

As the last golden rays of the sun touched the clouds in the western sky, there came the muffled beat of drums near by. David, waiting between Strong Wind and Little Bear outside the tepee, felt a quick surge of excitement.

Far down between the tepees he could see a procession of a dozen braves pacing slowly toward them in single file. Fading sunlight gleamed on naked copper flesh. Streaks of blue and scarlet paint stood out on foreheads and cheeks. Eagle feathers showed white against long black hair.

The muffled beat of the drums quickened. The marching column reached the tepee. One by one the warriors entered. When all were inside, Strong Wind motioned the boys in after him. He led David to a buffalo robe, and the boy sat down, acutely aware of the staring black eyes of the braves seated in a circle around the fire.

Strong Wind sat down on the boy's right, with Little Bear on his other side. As Singing Water and Pale Fawn and Run Lightly entered with long wooden platters of smoking buffalo ribs, David watched curiously. The braves sat unmoving, eyes on their chief. Strong Wind drew a long bone knife from his waist and cut off a chunk of meat. Intoning a few solemn words, he tossed the meat into the fire. The flames spluttered and flared. The offering to the Great Spirit made, bone knives were drawn out, and the braves fell to eating.

David pulled out his own hunting knife. Firelight flashed on the long steel blade. He felt the eyes of the Indians upon him. He looked up, abashed, but met the friendly looks of Standing Wolf and Star Watcher from across the circle. Shyly he smiled at them, then bit into the juicy meat.

When the feast was ended, Strong Wind shredded tobacco and red willow bark and filled the ceremonial pipe. Lighting it with a coal, he rose. Holding the bowl in both hands, he pointed the stem toward the heavens, then in turn toward the east, south, west, north. Last, he pointed the stem toward the earth. He took a few quick puffs on the pipe, then handed it to the nearest warrior and sat down.

The pipe passed around the circle. The braves talked and laughed as they smoked. Only when the last man had smoked did the chief interrupt. Raising one hand for silence, he addressed the council.

"We make feast for white boy, Daveed. White

boy risk life to help Little Bear. Wagon chief say no help Indian boy. Wagon chief angry when white boy disobey. Strike white boy."

The circle of braves listened intently, dark eyes glancing from their chief to the white boy.

"Strong Wind make white boy good present," the chief continued. "Give him Blue Thunder."

The braves murmured knowingly.

"Wagon chief try take Blue Thunder from white boy. Say Blue Thunder belong to him."

The Indians muttered angrily.

"White boy run away. Come to tepee of Strong Wind. Know Strong Wind his friend. White boy stay here now. Be Indian boy."

Standing Wolf spoke. "Indians friends of white boy," he acknowledged slowly. "What about Wagon chief? He angry, maybe come get white boy. Make bad medicine."

Strong Wind shook his head. "Scout come from Fort Laramie tonight. Wagon train gone on. Leave white boy. Wagon chief no want white boy catch up."

David gazed dazedly into the fire. He felt stunned. Bart had deliberately pushed on early, so that he could not come back. Now he was completely cut off from his own people. He bit his lower lip to stop its trembling.

Strong Wind caught the desolation in the boy's

face. He touched David's shoulder gently. "No worry. Daveed with friends."

David smiled up at him gratefully. "I know you're my friend, Chief Strong Wind. You make me good present. Now I want to make Strong Wind good present."

He got up and fetched his pouch from the back of the tepee. Kneeling down before the chief, he opened it and lifted out the bundle wrapped in his kerchief. While the braves craned their necks to see, he held out the bundle to the chief.

Strong Wind slowly unwrapped the kerchief. When he saw the twelve eagle feathers, an exclamation of pleasure escaped him. He held them up for all to see. The braves murmured admiringly.

The chief caressed the glossy quills with gentle fingers. "Daveed make good present," he said approvingly. "Where Daveed get feathers of golden eagle?"

"When the wagon train camped at Scott's Bluff, I climbed a cliff and found an eagle's nest," the boy explained. "When the big eagle came back to the nest, I shot him."

"White boy make brave deed to kill eagle on nest," Strong Wind told him.

Star Watcher spoke for the first time. "If white boy live in tepee of Strong Wind and be Indian boy," he said slowly, "White boy need Indian name."

Strong Wind looked at the other braves. One by one they nodded agreement.

The chief looked last at Standing Wolf. Standing Wolf nodded assent. "When son of Strong Wind make brave deed and kill bear with bow and arrow," he said in his deliberate way, "he get new Indian name, Little Bear. White boy make brave deed when he kill eagle. Let him have Indian name for brave deed."

Strong Wind nodded thoughtfully. "Daveed is white boy. He brave to kill golden eagle in nest. Now he dwell in tepee of Strong Wind and be brother to Little Bear. Let his Indian name be White Eagle, my second son."

And so David became White Eagle, second son of Chief Strong Wind. That night he slept on a buffalo robe beside Little Bear. They were up before dawn next morning. After they had eaten, they went outside. The coolness of dawn still lay on the prairie. Low fleecy clouds slowly tinged pink with the rising sun.

David drew a deep ecstatic breath. His blue eyes eagerly scanned the tepees near by. Outside, women bent over cooking fires. Braves lounged indolently before the open flaps of the tepees, smoking, calling to each other.

Slowly a look of disappointment crept into David's face. "Won't there be a hunt today?" he asked Little Bear anxiously.

Strong Wind emerged from the tepee in time to hear his question. "Hunt, White Eagle?"

"A buffalo hunt," the boy said eagerly. "I was hoping I could try out Blue Thunder."

A smiled tugged at Strong Wind's lips, but he answered the boy gravely. "A buffalo hunt is not simple, Second Son. Can White Eagle ride Blue Thunder without rein? Can he shoot thunder-stick from running pony?"

David's mouth dropped open. "I've—I've never tried," he stammered.

Strong Wind laid his hands on the boy's shoulders. "White Eagle must learn many things before he hunts buffalo. Come, we will bring up the ponies from the pasture, so that Little Bear may ride with us. We will seek out Black Hawk. Black Hawk will show White Eagle."

They brought up the horses from the pasture. Strong Wind lifted Little Bear onto Fleet Deer. "Bring the thunderstick," he directed David.

Slowly they rode down through the tepees.

"Who is Black Hawk?" David murmured to Little Bear.

"Chief of the Dog Soldiers, White Eagle. He and his soldiers guard the village. It was one of them who brought you in yesterday. They keep order in the village."

"Like sheriffs?" David asked.

Little Bear shook his head puzzledly. It was Strong Wind who answered.

"No one can leave village unless Black Hawk says. No one can hunt unless he says. Black Hawk great warrior, great hunter. He chief of hunt."

David nodded uncertainly. They were approaching the outskirts of the village. Fifty yards beyond the last tepee, a solitary brave sat motionless on a wiry black pony. The brave was tall and sinewy. Three eagle feathers were thrust upright in his long black hair. An ugly-looking rawhide quirt dangled from his right wrist.

As they approached, the brave rode to meet them. He and the chief spoke together rapidly in Sioux. From time to time the brave turned to glance at David. The boy shifted uncomfortably. He could see the twinkle in the round black eyes. The brave was laughing at him.

At last Strong Wind turned to them. "Black Hawk show White Eagle how Indian hunts buffalo. He use rabbit. Come."

Black Hawk drew his bow from his shoulder

and strung it. Then he led the way out onto the prairie at a fast lope. Almost out of sight of the village he reined up. Leaning down, he loosened the jaw rope from his pony and tossed it to Strong Wind.

"Isn't he going to use any rein at all?" David asked incredulously.

The chief shook his head. "Indians train ponies to guide with legs. Use hands for bow and arrow. Watch."

Black Hawk kicked his pony into a slow gallop, circling around and around through the sagebrush. Suddenly a long-eared rabbit flashed out of the brush and sped away over the prairie in high, sailing bounds. Black Hawk's pony leaped after him, swerving to come up on the rabbit's right side. Black Hawk jerked an arrow from his quiver and notched it to the bowstring. The bow bent. There was the flash of the arrow. The rabbit jerked in midair, then thudded to the ground.

The whole thing had happened so fast that David sat stunned. Dazedly he watched Black Hawk lean down from his pony and scoop up the rabbit by the shaft of the arrow. The chief of the Dog Soldiers rode back to where they watched.

"White boy try with thunderstick?" he asked smilingly.

David shook his head. "No use trying," he said

[99]

unhappily. "I couldn't ride bareback without a rein. I couldn't shoot my rifle, much less reload, just holding with my knees."

Black Hawk studied the boy's unhappy face. "I see white men shoot thunderstick many times at Fort Laramie. Thunderstick good on ground. Shoot far. No good on running pony. Indian shoot ten arrows while white man load."

David nodded thoughtfully.

"Strong Wind say second son want to be buffalo hunter. Black Hawk teach him. White Eagle like?"

David's eyes began to shine. "Oh, yes!" he cried. "I want to learn to ride and hunt like an Indian. I want to learn to be a good buffalo hunter!"

And so it happened that Black Hawk, chief of the Dog Soldiers, became David's teacher. Every day Black Hawk took the boys out on their horses. Day after day under his watchful eye David practiced riding Blue Thunder without rein, guiding him with the pressure of his knees, with the shifting weight of his body. Day after day the boy practiced doggedly with bow and arrow. Slowly he learned, until the day finally came when Black Hawk nodded wth satisfaction.

"Now White Eagle ride and shoot like Indian. White Eagle make good buffalo hunter."

David glowed at his words. In his heart the boy was not so sure. There were so many things to remember. The hunter must always approach the game from the right, so that he will be in the best position to draw back the arrow. He must aim always for the vulnerable spot just back of the right shoulder. He must learn to ride with a long rein looped around Blue Thunder's lower jaw, the loose end coiled and fastened to his own belt. Never was he to touch this long rein, unless unseated when the stallion dodged away from the savage horns of a wounded buffalo. Then he could grab the rein as it played out and not lose his horse.

It seemed too much to remember. Haltingly he tried, in the Sioux he had learned, to express his fears. Black Hawk only smiled.

"White Eagle has learned well. He will not forget."

The long summer days were never long enough. Every day David practiced with Blue Thunder, Little Bear patiently keeping him company. Then there were games with the other boys in the village. David and Little Bear were the only boys their age, but there were many slightly younger, and with these they swam and fished and wrestled and raced their horses.

David had lost all count of time. Never had he felt better. His muscles had tightened. His body had filled out. The hot summer sun had bleached his hair. His skin was bronzed. When he had time to think at all, the past seemed like a dream—his Grandma and Missouri and Uncle Andrew—the wagon train and Bart and old Amos.

The women in the village had finished scraping and stretching the buffalo skins from the last hunt. David liked to watch them work the skins, pulling them back and forth across ropes of braided sinews stretched taut from saplings and pegged into the ground.

"Make soft," Little Bear explained to his white brother. "Pound clay in. Make white. Skins for new winter tepees."

The thin sheets of buffalo meat that had hung drying on the racks were being taken down by the women. Patiently they pounded the dried meat into powder, mixing it with crushed chokecherries, moistening it with melted marrow. When it was finished, they stuffed the meat into skins for storing.

"It's good," David told Singing Water when she gave him a taste. "What's its name?"

"Pemmican," she smiled, "our food for long journeys and for winter."

Afterwards David was never sure of when he

first felt tension building up in the village. He knew that game was getting scarce. Rabbits and antelope were becoming harder to find. No buffalo herd had come near the village since David's arrival. More and more often there was no fragrance of roasting meat over the cooking fires at night. More and more often in the tepee of Strong Wind pemmican was all there was to eat.

Strong Wind said nothing to show that he worried, but David noticed the grim look on his face as he and the other braves returned day after day empty-handed from the hunt.

"Why doesn't the village move on to where we can find game?" David asked Little Bear one evening.

"I heard our father say that the time is not yet right," Little Bear told him. "He-Who-Speaks-Wisely, our shaman, makes prayers to the Great Spirit, but the Great Spirit has not spoken."

"What happens if the pemmican runs out before the Great Spirit speaks?" David asked practically.

Little Bear shrugged. "I do not believe this will happen. The Great Spirit will send the buffalo, so that we may have food. You will see."

The days passed. Night and day scouts scoured the prairie for buffalo sign. The Indians rested their ponies, letting them fatten before the hunting. All day long the men worked patiently at making new arrowheads. Each day there were smaller portions of pemmican in the wooden bowls. There was no singing or dancing in the village at night.

David spent more and more time out in the pasture with Blue Thunder. Hour after hour he spent teaching the stallion to come running to his whistle. Patiently he brushed the pale gray coat until it gleamed, combed the long black mane and tail free of tangles. Between the boy and the stallion there had grown up a deep love. Blue Thunder followed at his heels, like a puppy, when David wandered through the village.

Late one afternoon David was out in the pasture with the stallion, when suddenly he heard a great commotion in the village. The boy raced toward the tepees to see what had happened. He found the village in an uproar.

"The scouts have discovered a great buffalo herd!" Little Bear shouted, jumping up and down with excitement. "Our father has bidden the crier make the rounds. We move our village at dawn!"

The Buffalo Hunt

10

David and Little Bear were too excited to sleep much that night. They were up before dawn. While Little Bear was driving up the pack ponies from the pasture, David shinned up a pole to the top of the tepee and pulled out the pins that held the skins together. He and Singing Water folded the skins into a big bundle. Then they took down the tepee poles and lashed them together, two by two, for shafts for the travois.

By the time they had finished, Little Bear had tightened the leather cinches on the pack ponies. He and David lashed the pole shafts to the cinches, one on each side, the ends of the long poles dragging on the ground. Singing Water stretched buffalo skins over the shafts. Onto these litters she piled the household furnishings.

At last all was ready. David and Little Bear bridled Blue Thunder and Fleet Deer and herded the rest of the ponies of Strong Wind up from the pasture.

All over the plain where the village had stood loaded ponies waited patiently beside the blackened circles of dead cooking fires. Even the big dogs were harnessed into small travois. On the dog litters were the round leather bull boats, used for ferrying across rivers. The bull boats were piled high with leather storage bags from the households.

Strong Wind came up from the bank of the stream where he had been conferring with the old men of the tribe. "The old ones are ready to lead out," he told his family. "Come, let us take our place at the head of the procession."

One by one the families of the tribe moved into their proper places in the line. At the head waited a group of old men, silent and immobile in their long white buffalo robes.

"They will lead the tribe to the buffalo," Little Bear whispered to David. "All night they have made good medicine in the tepee of the shaman, our medicine man."

"Where are their horses?" David whispered.

"They do not ride. They walk. That is the Indian way."

The old men stood patiently waiting, faces toward the east. Behind them the Indians stood quietly beside their ponies and travois. The eastern sky lightened. Streaks of gold and crimson showed the coming of the sun. As the fiery tip appeared above the horizon the leader of the old men took three slow paces forward. From beneath his buffalo robe he drew out the ceremonial pipe. Lighting the pipe and cradling the bowl with both hands, he began to chant the prayer for guidance from the Great Spirit on the buffalo hunt. The wail of the chant rose and fell. Still holding the pipe with both hands, the old man raised it high, stem pointing toward the sky, then pointing, in turn, to the east, south, west, north, and finally down toward the earth.

When he was done he smoked, then passed the pipe to each of the old men. When all had smoked, the leader put the pipe away. With measured steps the old men led out southward along the stream, the long procession following in a straggly line.

David rode knee to knee with Little Bear, directly behind Strong Wind and Singing Water. The white boy's heart hammered with excitement. They were starting on a buffalo hunt.

All that day they crept southward across the prairie. The hot sun beat down upon them. Dust rose thick from the grass that stood belly high on the ponies. At sundown they reached the bank of a wide clear river. The old men who had led the march sat down beneath a tall cottonwood, signifying they would make camp there.

The women bustled about, unpacking their travois on the sites reserved for their families. Soon the great double circle of tepees was erected. Cooking fires crackled. Ponies were hobbled and turned loose to graze.

David and Little Bear hobbled Strong Wind's twelve ponies, then rubbed down their horses with bunches of coarse grass.

"Tomorrow," said Little Bear, "when we start after buffalo, we will ride common ponies and lead our runners until we reach the herd. Then our runners will be fresh."

While they were working, a scout galloped in

and stopped before the tepee of Black Hawk. All over camp braves dropped what they were doing and ran to hear the news he had brought.

"Come!" Little Bear cried to David. "Now Black Hawk will give orders to the hunters for tomorrow."

The boys raced across the prairie toward the tepee of the leader of the Dog Soldiers. They wormed their way through the crowd. Black Hawk was speaking.

"We ride out before dawn," he was saying. "Picket your runners before the tepees. Look to your weapons."

The men hastened away to bring up their runners. Women led the common ponies up close to the village, where they could be easily caught. Every brave hurried to his tepee to check his bow and arrows.

Strong Wind and the two boys were soon finished. They were standing outside the tepee when Black Hawk, flanked by two Dog Soldiers, walked down toward them. David recognized Black Hawk's companions. They were Silver Beaver and Running Antelope, group leaders for the hunt. The white boy gazed fascinatedly at the heavy clubs the braves carried.

The three halted before the chief. Black Hawk spoke. "White Eagle, second son of Strong Wind, is permitted to go on his first buffalo hunt tomorrow. Strong Wind must instruct him in the rules of the hunt."

The chief nodded gravely, turning to David. "White Eagle, my second son, this is the first time since you have been with us that the entire tribe hunts the buffalo. Know, then, that this hunt is different from the individual hunt, when each brave hunts for himself. We ride against a great buffalo herd. Such a herd can be stampeded very easily. One over-eager brave may do this and may thereby cause the whole tribe to starve. You understand what I say to you?"

David nodded solemnly. "I understand, Second Father."

"Good. You know that Black Hawk is the chief of the hunt. He is a stern leader. Every man must obey his rules, even I. Each hunter must have equal chance with all others. If any disobeys, Black Hawk will flog him with his quirt without mercy. He will break his weapons, will send him back to the village in disgrace. I would not have this for my son."

David shivered at the solemn words. "I promise I will obey Black Hawk's orders, Second Father."

Strong Wind looked straight into David's eyes. "This is all new to you, White Eagle. Yet I have confidence in you. You must watch Black Hawk's signals. When the chase starts, there will be no one to help you."

He stopped. Black Hawk looked at the boys keenly. "Remember to choose a fat cow for your target," he told them. "Ride fearlessly into the herd. Send your pony close up on the right side of the buffalo. Send your arrow through the ribs, just back of the shoulder. If you hit the life spot, you may kill with one arrow. If not, you will have to use more. Watch the buffalo. They are very quick, very strong. They can hook their horns under a pony's belly and toss him high in the air. Many men have been killed."

There was little sleep in the village that night. Some men prayed until dawn in the tepee of the shaman. Fires were kept burning in all tepees, sending showers of sparks belching up out of smokeholes.

Before dawn the camp came alive. Stars shone pale as the hunters rode out, leading their runners, to where the Dog Soldiers waited on the edge of the village. In the grayness before dawn all hunters looked alike. Each wore breechclout and moccasins. Each had a quiver of arrows over his shoulder, a bow in his hand.

At Black Hawk's command they set out in a loose group behind the soldiers. David rode between Strong Wind and Little Bear. His heart beat fast with excitement.

Mile after mile they covered at a slow gallop. The sky paled in the east, then glowed crimson and gold as the sun rose, flooding the prairie with yellow light.

They reached the side of a hill where the scouts waited. At Black Hawk's signal the hunters halted at the foot of the hill. Each hunter sprang from his tired pony and leaped upon his fresh runner. Bows were strung and arrows loosened in the quivers.

Black Hawk's keen eyes swept the band, found David. "White Eagle, come," he commanded.

The astonished boy rode after Black Hawk and his two group leaders, Silver Beaver and Running Antelope, up the steep hill. They reined up on top. David gasped in wonder. Below on the prairie as far as eye could see a huge buffalo herd grazed peacefully.

Great shaggy bulls cropped the grass on the outskirts of the herd. Sleek fat cows fed in the center, their awkward yellow calves chasing in and out through the herd, racing back on clumsy legs to bunt their heads against their mothers' flanks. Here and there brash young bulls charged one another head-on, crashing together with wild bellows, testing their strength.

Black Hawk sat studying the terrain. To their left the prairie valley was bordered by low hills. He turned to Silver Beaver and pointed toward the hills. "Divide the hunters in two parties. Take one party and circle around behind those hills until you outflank the herd on the far side. When you arrive, and are lined up, Running Antelope will bring the rest of the hunters up from the foot of the hill here. We will attack at the same time from both sides."

Silver Beaver and Running Antelope rode swiftly down the hill. Quickly Silver Beaver picked out thirty hunters. He signaled them to follow him. They galloped away to the left and vanished back of the hills.

Black Hawk and David watched from the hill-top. Through the openings between the hills they caught glimpses of the galloping ponies. At last the hunters circled the herd and arrived at the far side. They spread out in a line flanking the herd, awaiting Black Hawk's signal.

At the base of the hill the rest of the hunters stretched out in a long line. At a signal from Black Hawk they sent their ponies forward side by side up the hill. When they reached the top Black Hawk took his place at the front. He gave a second signal. They rode over the crest and down the slope toward the buffalo at a swift gallop. At the same instant from the far side of the valley, Silver Beaver and his party raced out across the plain. The two lines of hunters rushed down toward the grazing herd.

Shaggy bulls on the fringe caught the man smell. Bellowing and roaring, they wheeled and crashed into the herd. Bleating calves and screaming cows were trampled under the hoofs of the fear-crazed bulls.

The hunters were quirting their runners, each determined to be first. Black Hawk, followed by David, raced ahead of the line of braves. David was pushing Blue Thunder into the herd, dodging the big bulls, forcing the stallion forward toward the fat cows in the center. The yelling, whooping hunters split the herd in a dozen places. The panicked buffalo turned in headlong flight.

Blue Thunder was well into the herd. David glanced about grimly. On every side was a seething, tossing wave of giant brown bodies. The thunder of hoofs was deafening. Dust rolled up, blinding the boy. A suddenly uptossed horn grazed his left knee. Hot blood ran down his leg. He could not shoot. The buffalo crowded too close.

On and on they thundered. Suddenly a gap opened up on the left. Blue Thunder swerved through. He was racing neck and neck with a fat cow. David jerked an arrow from his quiver. He notched it to his bow. Drawing the arrow back to his shoulder, he loosed it. The twang was lost in the thunder of hoofs. The arrow went into the cow's shoulder almost up to the feathers.

David shot again. The second arrow hit lower than the first. The cow did not falter. The boy's breath was coming in shallow gasps. He sent a third arrow, a fourth.

Suddenly the cow's head swung around with a savage swipe of horns. Blue Thunder dodged. David felt searing pain in his right leg as the stallion smashed against the buffalo running beside him.

Blue Thunder swerved off. Grimly David notched an arrow to his bow. Blood was pouring from the nose of the wounded cow. The bow string twanged. The arrow went in to the feathers just behind the shoulder. The cow reared up with a maddened bellow. Then the big body crashed heavily into the path of Blue Thunder.

The stallion hit the huge carcass with a jar that flung David forward against the horse's neck. The bow flew out of the boy's hand. He grabbed frantically for Blue Thunder's mane as the stallion stumbled to his knees on top of the shaggy carcass.

Blue Thunder squealed in terror. He reared, pivoted, and leaped around the carcass, galloping on, surrounded by a seething, tossing wave of brown backs.

Slowly David pushed himself upright. He was trembling. Dazedly he peered through the dust, searching for a way out of the panicked herd. Off to his right he glimpsed Silver Beaver, lashing his pony on after a big bull. Then pony and rider vanished into the dust cloud.

Suddenly the agonized scream of a horse rose shrill above the thunder of hoofs. David jerked around. The wounded bull had turned on his pursuer, had impaled Silver Beaver's pony on his horns. High into the air pony and rider were lifted across the head of the bull. Silver Beaver clung helplessly to the mane of his pony as they were carried along on the horns of the maddened bull.

Cold sweat broke out over David's body. The pony was slipping sideways down over the bull's neck. Suddenly Silver Beaver threw himself into the air. He hit the ground, rolled over and over, then bounded to his feet and raced out of the path of the stampeding herd.

Blue Thunder swept on, pocketed by plunging, shaggy brown humps. The pound of hoofs was like the angry rumble of thunder. The herd was a maddened, seething mass of confusion. Arrows flashed in the sunlight. Buffalo went down, great sprawling, kicking masses of flesh.

The rush of the stampede swept the stallion on for a quarter of a mile before David could edge him out of the herd. David pulled him up with shaking hands. The stallion was streaked with lather. He stood with legs spraddled, sides heaving.

The boy was trembling violently. Dazedly he sat and watched the hunt stream past until at last there were only a few straggling old bulls galloping along clumsily in the wake of the herd. Slowly the dust settled. The plain was dotted with huge brown bodies. Cautiously the boy touched the stallion forward in and out between the fallen giants, seeking his arrows. He found them at last. He looked down at the fat sleek cow. His face burned when he counted the five arrows. He slid to the ground.

Suddenly a voice spoke from behind him. "White Eagle kill first buffalo. Little Bear kill first buffalo."

David whirled. Strong Wind and Little Bear had ridden up noiselessly behind him. They smiled down at him, their faces and bodies streaked with sweat and dirt.

"It took me five arrows," David said embarrassedly. "That's not very good. Besides, I lost my bow."

"I shot four arrows," Little Bear consoled him.

"For first hunt, it is not bad," Strong Wind told them. "You will do better next time."

All over the trampled plain Indians returning from the chase rode slowly in and out among the carcasses, searching out the arrows that bore the signs of their names. A horde of boys had ridden up from the village. The hunters slid off their tired runners and turned them over to the boys, then set to the skinning at once. Knives flashed. Skins rolled back. The air was heavy with the smell of fresh blood.

They had no more than started when the Squaw Train arrived, a long line of pack ponies dragging travois and carrying the women and children. They jumped off their ponies and darted through the crowd, seeking out their men. Crying out joyfully when they spied them, the women took over the butchering, bringing their men tidbits of raw liver, sprinkled with gall, to refresh them.

It did not take the women long to cut the meat from the bones with their quick, sure strokes. Liver and kidneys and heart and tongue they set aside carefully, as great delicacies. When they had finished with one buffalo, they threw the skin, hair side down, on travois or on pack ponies, packed the meat on top, turned up the hide, and lashed it on with stout rawhide thongs. Then they moved on, searching out another buffalo holding the arrows of their tepees.

It was sunset when the long line of ponies returned to the village with their burdens of buffalo. The old women had the long drying racks ready. The meat was unloaded. Cooking fires crackled.

To Standing Wolf and to Star Watcher fell the task of giving out meat to the tepees of those too old to hunt. David and Little Bear helped in the distributing. Afterwards, in the tepee of Strong Wind, with Singing Water roasting the juicy hump ribs over the cooking fire, with Little Bear stroking the hide of his buffalo and chattering happily, David fell silent.

Strong Wind noticed. "White Eagle does not rejoice over the buffalo which make our people happy," he said gently. "What is it that troubles you, Second Son? What causes you to look far away, and with sadness?"

"I'm not sad," David protested. "I'm happy over the buffalo." He hesitated. "It was the old mothers in the tepees where we carried the gift meat," he said finally. "They reminded me of my Grandma, the old mother in my tepee back home in Missouri."

"White Eagle longs for his own people?"

David shook his head. "I'm happy with you here in the village, Second Father. I don't want to go home. Not yet," he added honestly. "I was just wishing my Grandma and my Uncle Andrew could see my first buffalo," he finished with a grin. "They would be proud."

Night came. All over the village cooking fires sputtered and flared under the roasting meat. When the feasting was done, the loud pulsing beat of the drums and the shrill buzz of the rattles called the people for the dances and the songs of thanksgiving.

A huge fire leaped in the center of the village. Musicians sat in an arc at the outer edge of the great circle. Indians were packed solidly around the circle, watching and waiting. Suddenly the drums muted, muttering softly. The crowd parted. Into the open stepped He-Who-Speaks-Wisely. Pacing slowly toward the fire, he stopped beside it. The crowd grew quiet. The shaman began to sing, the words of his singing telling the story of the need of his people, telling the story of his prayers to Wahkan-Tanka, the Great Spirit, telling of the smile of Wahkan-Tanka upon their hunt that day.

When he had finished, the drums quickened, pulsing, throbbing. A stir of excitement swept the watching Indians. Out into the circle stepped the young men who had killed their first buffalo that day. Firelight gleamed on naked bodies as they bent in the stomping rhythm of the dance. Firelight glistened on long black hair, and on the yellow hair of White Eagle, who danced for the first time with his adopted brothers, the Sioux.

On the Trail

11

The hunt was over. There was an air of festivity throughout the village. Cooking fires crackled. All day long there was the tantalizing aroma of roasting meat. The hunters, rested after the dancing, moved from tepee to tepee, feasting and smoking and recounting their tales of the buffalo.

From sunrise to sunset the women labored

busily, laughing and chattering as they cut meat into long strips and hung them on racks for the drying, working three and four together at pegging and scraping and sanding the hides.

As the days passed, bags made of tripe and filled with pemmican hung from poles in the tepees. Beside them hung the larger bags, made from the skin of the buffalo, holding dried meat. Even in the tepees of the old, where no hunter dwelled, there was meat enough for a long time to come.

Days were growing shorter. Nights were cold. Now the women began to hurry. They gathered together each morning with the hides for the winter tepees, and sinews and awls made from the wing bones of eagles. All day long they sewed the skins together.

Every day Little Bear and David hunted. Antelope was plentiful, and occasionally the boys rode upon straggling buffalo that they ran with their horses.

"The buffalo know that the snows are coming," Little Bear told his white brother one day when they had brought down a young buffalo bull. "See how thick and glossy the bull's fur has grown? Soon we shall travel to the Black Hills, White Eagle. Then we shall have the Fall Hunt. That is the best hunt of all."

"Everybody keeps talking about the winter camp in the Black Hills, Little Bear. Do you go there every winter?"

"But of course. On the prairie close to the hills, the great herd journeys south for the winter. That is when we have our big hunt. And even after the herd has passed southward, many buffalo winter in the hills to escape the blizzards on the prairie. There will be fresh meat in plenty."

David's eyes sparkled. "When do you think we'll start?"

"Soon. Our father says that the shaman prays even now for word from the Great Spirit. Soon the skins for our winter tepees will be finished. Soon we shall begin our journey.

Two weeks later Strong Wind lingered long in the tepee of the shaman one evening. Before he returned to his own tepee, David and Little Bear heard the voice of the crier from far down in the village. They dashed outside, almost colliding with Strong Wind in the doorway.

"What is it, our father?" Little Bear cried.

"The shaman has announced that the time is right for our journey to the Black Hills," Strong Wind told them. "We set out at sunrise."

Singing Water joined them. "Soon we shall cut

poles for our new winter tepees," she said joyfully.

"Soon we shall go on the Fall Hunt!" Little Bear told her. "The buffalo fur will be thick and glossy. They will give us much trade in the spring at Fort Laramie. I will buy a thunderstick, and White Eagle will teach me to shoot it."

Strong Wind and Singing Water went into the tepee. The boys sat down outside. In the distance came the rise and fall of the voice of the crier. David looked up at the stars. Already he had three buffalo pelts in the tepee, but he wanted more, many more. There was Grandma to think of, back home in Missouri. And there was Blue Thunder. Just thinking of the stallion sent a warm glow through the boy's body. Blue Thunder should have the finest saddle he could buy, a saddle worthy of the noble stallion.

"What are you thinking of?" Little Bear asked curiously.

David came back with a start. "Of the Black Hills," he lied. "Where are they, Little Bear? How far away?"

"Many camps away," Little Bear replied. "Our trail lies somewhere between the north star and the rising sun."

. . .

[125]

By sunrise next morning the tepees were down and folded, the ponies brought up from the pasture, the travois piled high with the goods of the households. After the old men had blessed the journey, the villagers moved out across the prairie. For a quarter of a mile the barren plain was scattered over by braves on horseback, pack ponies, dog travois, women and old men plodding doggedly through the tall grass on foot, children chasing in and out among the crowd.

All that long hot day they crept slowly across the dreary monotony of prairie. That night they pitched their tepees beside a shallow stream, half choked with rank grass, where great green bullfrogs croaked a hoarse chorus all night long, and swarms of night bugs droned in the tepees, plaguing their sleep.

Next morning they reached the Platte. The river was almost a mile wide at the crossing, its muddy water no more than a foot deep, except for occasional holes washed out deep in the sandy bottom. The turgid water flowed sluggishly in and around many islands of cottonwoods and willows.

The Indians swarmed down the bank in noisy confusion. Bull boats, round shallow boats made of buffalo skins, were unloaded, and household goods ferried across by their owners, who splashed along beside the boats, swimming when they encountered deep holes, then returning with empty boats for another load.

Little Bear and David crossed over and back six times, helping Singing Water ferry their belongings in the bull boat. Then they returned for their horses and helped Strong Wind drive the common ponies across, careful to keep them clear of treacherous quicksand.

On the north bank the travois were reloaded, and they set out once again across the wide prairie.

Day after day they pushed north and east, crossing the treacherous Niobrara at the lower ford, where the icy water raced swiftly past tree-covered islands and the horses floundered with panicked lunges through clinging quicksand.

Gradually the plains gave way to ridges and flats and deep gullies. It was not until they had left the Cheyenne behind them, however, that they came within sight of the hills; and by then both people and horses were weary and worn from the journey.

On the first foothill slopes that led up from the prairie, they camped on the bank of a swift mountain stream. Soon the great circle of tepees stood sheltered by the tall pines that grew thick in the foothills.

"We shall dwell here until the snows of winter are melted," Strong Wind announced. "There will be fish enough in the stream, and game in the forest. We are close to the prairie. The great herd of buffalo will pass our way."

All the rest of that day men and boys stretched flat beside the swift stream. In their hands they held nooses, braided from hairs from the tails of their ponies. They fished without talking. Many trout were jerked from the water, flopping wildly on the bank, their speckled bellies glistening in the sunlight, until a blow on the head with a rock stilled their struggles.

Little Bear and David bore five big trout home in triumph, scaled and gutted and wrapped in wet moss. Singing Water broiled the trout over hot coals, and they feasted.

"The fish please, after days of pemmican," Strong Wind told them when they had eaten.

"White Eagle and I will bring in fresh meat tomorrow," Little Bear promised. "We saw antelope today back down on the prairie. White Eagle will take his thunderstick. Perhaps we shall kill a fine buck."

There was singing and dancing in the village that evening. The people rejoiced that they had left behind the heat and dust of the prairie.

At sunrise next morning Little Bear and David caught their horses. They followed the stream down out of the foothills. On the level plain the stream widened, grew shallow, flowed lazily between low banks thick with willows.

David and Little Bear knew exactly where they were going. The day before the tribe had passed the mouth of a wide draw that curved back around a bluff, like a horseshoe. The stream flowed through the center. On each side of the water was a wide grassy flat, five hundred yards across, and beyond the flats were precipitous bluffs that shut in the draw from the prairie.

"There will be many antelope coming to drink," Little Bear called now, as they galloped along.

David nodded. "It's the only running water anywhere around. How much farther, Little Bear?"

"One mile, perhaps two. We must not ride into the draw, White Eagle. Our horses would frighten any antelope that might be at the water."

The plain was cut now with long shallow draws and basins. They swung away left from the stream and sent the horses cautiously up over the rough ground. Ahead they could see the uneven rim of the draw.

"Better we walk now," Little Bear said in a low voice.

They tied the horses to a cedar and stole through the sagebrush, their moccasins noiseless on the hard packed earth. They reached the rim of the draw and crouched down behind clumps of sage.

"Look!" Little Bear said.

Down in the draw two hundred yards to their left a big buck antelope stood motionless atop a low hummock, his head lifted toward the flat across the stream. Suddenly a second buck emerged from the sagebrush beyond the water. He stopped. For a long moment the bucks faced each other across the stream. Then suddenly the second buck wheeled and disappeared into the sage.

"What are they up to?" David whispered.

"The old buck on this side guards his band. They are feeding in the brush back close to the cliff. The young buck across there would like to fight for the herd, but he is not big and strong enough yet, and does not dare."

The boys crouched motionless, watching the buck on the hummock. All at once from directly beneath them a third buck hove into view. Heavily pronged, the newcomer strutted pompously down the draw toward the buck standing guard.

The latter spotted the intruder at that moment.

His rump patch flashed white in the sunlight. His shrill whistle of alarm reached the boys faintly. He vanished from the hummock. The next instant he fled away up the draw at the head of a large band of does. The intruder buck sped after them, slim legs a misty blur under his body.

Up and around the curve of the stream the antelope raced, vanishing behind the tall bluff.

"Did you see them run!" David exclaimed.

"Fast," Little Bear nodded. "White Eagle! Look! Over the bluff where the antelope ran. An eagle!"

All David caught was the swoop of wide wings as the eagle dropped down behind the bluff. "You think he's after antelope?" he asked excitedly.

Little Bear nodded. "Come! Quickly!"

They started down the steep sandy bank, slipping and sliding. Halfway down they brought up against a big clump of sagebrush. At that instant the antelope band burst out from behind the bluff, flying down toward them. The eagle sailed low over the herd, keeping pace, his mighty wings sending him forward with long, powerful sweeps.

"They're coming right at us!" David gasped. He was pouring powder into his rifle. Quickly he rammed patch and ball home. "Get the buck out front, Little Bear!"

[131]

The boys plowed down through caving sand to the floor of the draw. The antelope were bearing down on them, a blur of racing bodies, flashing legs. The eagle had dropped down. He was flying not over ten feet above the buck out front, flying with talons outstretched, head down.

There was the drumming of flying hoofs, the white flashes of rump patches. The antelope were even with the boys. Suddenly the eagle folded his wings and dropped, talons wide, upon the neck of the buck. The buck went down kicking, throwing his horned head wildly from side to side.

There came the crack of a rifle. An arrow flashed. The buck's legs flailed once. The eagle fell clear. The great wings beat convulsively, then stilled. The antelope herd swept by in a cloud of dust.

When David and Little Bear rode back into camp, the Indians gathered around them with loud exclamations, gazing curiously at the buck draped across Fleet Deer, pointing at the gouges left by the eagle's talons on the back of his neck. Avidly they examined the great eagle held by David.

Strong Wind accepted the eagle with low grunts of pleasure. He ran his hand lightly over the rump of the fat buck. "My sons have hunted well," he announced to the people. "Meat for the tepee and the golden eagle for feathers and for claws." He spread the tail wide. "Feathers enough for a war bonnet!"

The Enemy Strikes

12

At sunrise the tribe rode far up onto the foothill slopes to where slender spruce grew thickly. They set to work with hatchets and knives, chopping down trees, trimming off branches, lashing the trunks into bundles to be dragged back down into camp.

All next day they labored at peeling the spruce

poles, measuring and cutting them into proper lengths, stacking the finished poles into upright cones for the drying.

David and Little Bear worked beside Singing Water. Strong Wind had helped with the cutting, as had all the braves, but while his wife and sons peeled and stacked, the chief sat at the door of the tepee, wrapping the quills of the eagle, preparing them for a new war bonnet.

The days sped by. When the lodge poles were seasoned, the women erected the new winter tepees, frugally saving the skins from the old and using them for moccasins and for storage bags.

The first frost came. The leaves of the aspen glowed gold against the dark green of pines on the hillside. Now when David and Little Bear rode out on their runners, the breath from the horses' nostrils left misty streamers on the cold air.

When the boys awoke one frosty morning, they found that Singing Water had laid out buckskin shirts and leggings for them to wear.

"These feel good, Second Mother," David told her gratefully. "Yesterday when we hunted, we wrapped our buffalo robes about us for warmth."

"The North Wind will bring the great buffalo herd down from their summer home," Strong

Wind told them. "They will pass close by our village on their way south to the cave of the Great Spirit. When they come, we will have our Fall Hunt. There will be meat enough in the tepees for winter."

Little Bear went to squat down beside him. "My father, White Eagle has not seen the hunting grounds of our old fathers," he said eagerly. "May we ride there today?"

Strong Wind hesitated. "Only last night Black Hawk reported that our scouts have seen the tracks of strange ponies on the prairie," he said slowly. "I do not know—"

"We will take care," Little Bear promised eagerly. "We will have sharp eyes for any enemy."

"Go then," Strong Wind said reluctantly. "Be back before the sun sets. Our Dog Soldiers will allow no one to approach after darkness falls."

Taking their bows and arrows and small pouches of pemmican, the boys caught their runners and set out down the bank of the stream. When they reached the prairie, they swung north. Mile after mile of sagebrush plain the horses covered at an easy gallop. Six or seven miles to the north they came to a shallow stream that flowed lazily southward between low bluffs. They rode down the crumbling bank onto the stretch of hard sand beside the water. The horses stretched out in a run.

They had not ridden a mile, when David called to Little Bear. "That dark line up ahead," he pointed. "It looks like the top of a mesa."

Little Bear shook his head. "That is the upper prairie, where we are going."

"Upper prairie?"

"Here, where we are now, is low prairie, White Eagle. Up ahead the low prairie ends in high bluffs. On top of the bluffs is prairie once more. That is what we call the upper prairie."

They rode on. On both sides of the bed of the stream the terrain grew rough, with broken cuts and dry washes leading up to sharp ridges. On their right the ridges gave way to steep hills. Ahead the bluffs loomed higher and higher, dark no longer, but red in the sunlight.

The river bed wound in and around rocky ridges. As they rounded a jutting boulder David reined up, staring openmouthed at piles of bleached bones that littered the banks of the stream.

"Buffalo bones!" he exclaimed. "Look at that big skull half buried in the sand!"

"This is the hunting ground of our old fathers," Little Bear told him. "Here, they butchered the buffalo they had killed. Look up ahead, White Eagle, there at the base of the bluff. What do you see?"

"It looks like some kind of big pen or corral," David said slowly. "All those logs fallen down—"

Little Bear nodded. "Built by our fathers, many, many snows past," he said. "Come, I will show you."

They got off their horses at the base of the bluff and scrambled up over the litter of fallen logs and tumbled boulders until they looked down inside the corral. Part of the wall was still standing. Inside was a piled-up jumble of bleached bones.

"How did they get them into the pen?" David asked.

"The buffalo trap is on top of the bluff," Little Bear told him.

"You mean they ran them over the cliff? How did they do it?"

"Long ago our tribe had no horses. It was very hard to kill buffalo on the prairie on foot. Our people built this trap."

"How did they get them into the trap?"

"Each tribe had a caller, a warrior with the gift from the Great Spirit for calling the buffalo, so they would listen. The caller wore a buffalo robe about his body and a hollow buffalo head over his head. When the buffalo grazed near the trap, he would show himself, would dance about, would call. Buffalo are very curious. They would follow the caller, coming faster and faster. At the edge of the bluff the caller would run out of their path, and they would race over the bluff."

"Can you still see the trap?"

"Yes. Look, there on the face of the bluff to your right. You can see the wide trail made by buffalo coming down from the upper prairie to the river. Come, we will ride up, and I will show you the trap."

They rode up the rocky trail that spiraled steeply up the face of the bluff. On top they rode out into a prairie valley a mile wide, shut in on the east by a high ridge.

"What are those mounds of rock fanning out from the bluff?" David asked curiously. "Somebody built them."

"That is the trap. The mounds are spaced the length of five horses. Let us ride to the top of the ridge. You can see the whole trap from there."

On top of the ridge they reined up. David studied the prairie valley below. The trap was a runway between two long lines of rock mounds that fanned out from the bluff in a huge V. At the edge of the bluff the trap narrowed to two hundred feet. Back up the valley the trap spread wider and wider as far as he could see.

"What kept the buffalo from running out between the mounds on each side?" David asked.

"Our people hid behind the mounds before the run commenced. They carried buffalo robes. When the herd ran past the mounds, the people jumped up, screaming and flapping the robes. That would frighten the buffalo and make them run faster."

"I wish I could have seen it," David sighed.

"Since our people have horses, they use the trap no longer," Little Bear told him. "Come, let us ride back down to the river and drink and eat."

"Wait!" David was staring toward the east, shading his eyes with his hand. "There on that high ridge. Smoke!"

Little Bear studied the puffs and spurts of black smoke that rose jerkily from the distant ridge. "It is a Pawnee signal fire," he said excitedly. "It says there is a great buffalo herd four camps to the north." He watched intently for a moment. "They have seen a Sioux village in the foothills," he said darkly. "They mean our village. Come, White Eagle, we must ride like the wind and bear this news to our father."

. . .

The guard was doubled around the village that night. Buffalo runners were picketed at the doors of the tepees. Nothing happened to disturb the sleep of the villagers. In the morning scouts were sent out. Toward sunset they returned. They had discovered the ashes of the Pawnee signal fire, they reported. Seven warriors had been in the party. The tracks of their ponies led east. The scouts had followed the tracks for miles, until the Pawnees had ridden outside the boundary of the hunting ground. Then they had turned back.

"They saw that we were too many for them," Black Hawk said proudly.

"I am not so sure," Strong Wind replied slowly. "The Pawnees are brave, and they are as sly as the gray wolf. I do not trust them."

Next day the men of the tribe sharpened and polished their arrows. While they worked, the women built drying racks for the meat they would bring home from the hunt.

At sunset their scouts rode in from the upper prairie. A herd so large that it stretched out of sight over the prairie was moving slowly down toward them. It was still a good three camps away.

There was singing and dancing in the village that night. Fires leaped high. Drums kept up a muffled beat. Firelight glinted on naked copper bodies as the warriors danced the welcome for the buffalo. Only Strong Wind held apart. He stood in the shadows, wrapped in his buffalo robe, dark eyes watching the dancers broodingly.

"Our father is not at peace, so long as Pawnees are near our hunting grounds," Little Bear whispered to David.

It was long past midnight when the village quieted. David and Little Bear fell asleep the moment they stretched out on their buffalo robes.

David came awake to the sound of loud shouts and the muffled thud of moccasined feet racing past the tepee. Little Bear was on his feet, staring wild-eyed at the door. Strong Wind and Singing Water were gone from the tepee.

The boys dashed outside, then pulled up short.

"Our runners," Little Bear shouted. "They are gone from their pickets!"

The village was in a turmoil. Men and women raced down between the tepees toward the horse pasture, shouting as they ran. Suddenly from a tepee close by a low moaning wail arose.

David's flesh crawled. "What's that?" he asked hoarsely.

"It is the wail for the dead," Little Bear cried.

"It comes from the tepee of Gray Beaver. He was horse guard this night. He's dead!"

Ahead, they could see a crowd gathered in the pasture. Suddenly the crowd parted, drew back. Four men, carrying the body of a brave, walked slowly up toward the tepees. David and Little Bear stepped aside. It was the body of Gray Beaver. David's stomach heaved. Gray Beaver had been scalped. The boy shut his eyes against the sight of the raw, bloody head.

The braves were past with their burden. There was a bitter, burning taste in David's mouth as he hurried after Little Bear toward where the tribe was gathered.

Strong Wind stood in front of the people. Beside him stood Black Hawk, holding the bridles of four shaggy ponies. Out in the trampled pasture, Standing Wolf and Star Watcher painstakingly studied the ground under the light of torches. The tribe waited tensely. David folded his arms against his chest to still their trembling. The horses had been stolen. His stallion was gone. A dry sob racked the boy's body.

Out in the pasture Standing Wolf and Star Watcher spoke briefly together, then turned toward the villagers. Standing Wolf addressed the chief.

"Seven men rode close to our village," he told him. "They tied their ponies beyond the clump of pines there at the edge of the pasture. They were Pawnees. We have found the tracks of their moccasins. One man crept up on Gray Beaver and killed him. We found the blood on the grass. Three entered our village and cut the picket ropes of our runners. They led them here. When they had cut the hobbles of the common ponies, they drove them off together, all but the four Black Hawk guards."

"How long ago?" Strong Wind asked.

"The tracks are still fresh. Not more than two hours. They are heading south."

An angry muttering growl welled up from the crowd.

Strong Wind raised his hand for silence. "Gray Beaver will be avenged," he said harshly. "Many Pawnee scalps will pay for his murder."

David swallowed convulsively, his eyes on the cold, stern face of his second father.

"The Pawnees cannot have ridden far, driving so many ponies," Strong Wind continued. "We must get our ponies back. Without them, we cannot kill buffalo. Without them, our people will starve."

He stopped. There was not a sound, not a movement. Then from far up the village came the

desolate wail of the widow of Gray Beaver. Somewhere a dog howled mournfully. A long shudder-
ing moan rose from the crowd.

"Our scouts still have their runners, but they
will need them," Standing Wolf said harshly.
"Give these four common ponies to me and Star
Watcher. We will follow the trail of our enemy
while it is still fresh. By changing ponies often,
we can overtake them before the sun sets again.
We will bring back our ponies, or else we will
die."

The tribe watched silently from the edge of the
village when the two warriors rode off on their
mission. Standing Wolf and Star Watcher had
donned war shirts and leggings. In their hair
they wore eagle feathers. Each carried bow and
arrows. Each carried a war spear. Under the red
and black paint on their cheeks, their faces were
grim and forbidding. As they rode southward,
each leading a second pony, the two warriors
chanted their war song. The villagers could hear
the sound of their chanting even after they had
vanished beyond the trees.

The Buffalo Caller

13

Morning came with leaden skies and the feel of snow in the air. The first frenzied shock at the loss of the horses had passed. All over the village braves stood at the doors of their tepees, silent and watchful.

Suddenly the muffled throb of a drum started

from the center of the village. Another and another picked up the thudding beat until the air was filled with the hollow, pulsing rhythm.

One by one, the braves stepped out from their tepees and stalked silently toward the council lodge.

David sat beside Little Bear at one side of the huge tepee, along with all young braves who had killed their first buffalo. His heart was heavy. In his hand was the frayed rope end from the picket of Blue Thunder.

Solemnly the warriors filed into the lodge and sat down around the sides, well back from the council, who sat with Strong Wind and the shaman in a half circle around the council fire.

The pipe was lighted. Not until every man around the council fire had smoked did Strong Wind speak.

"My people, today the council has invited all braves to meet here, so that all may ponder what is best for us to do. The great buffalo herd approaches. If we do not hunt, they will soon be gone from our hunting ground, without giving us meat for the winter. Standing Wolf and Star Watcher are brave warriors. They will recapture our ponies or will die. But we cannot sit idle and let the buffalo pass by on the prairie."

An old man in the council raised his head. His long braids were streaked with white. His face was netted with wrinkles.

"I was but a child when the Crows defeated our people and robbed us of our ponies," he said heavily, "yet I remember. The snows came. There was no food. We dug roots from the frozen earth to keep alive. Many starved. When the snows melted, there were no old ones and no babies in the tepees. Strong warriors died, too."

"I have heard the tale from my father," Strong Wind told him. "We must plan wisely, so that such suffering will not come to us now."

From the throng of men who sat next to the council a young warrior sprang to his feet. Two eagle feathers were thrust into his long black hair. Firelight glinted on hard black eyes, outlined the cruel downward thrust of thin lips, the livid scars that slanted down his right cheek. "I say a raid on the Pawnee village!" he cried. "We do not know that Standing Wolf and Star Watcher will return with our ponies. Let me lead a war party against the Pawnees! I will bring you ponies!"

"Yellow Fang speaks with the tongue of an infant," Strong Wind rebuked. "There is no time to make war on our enemies. The great herd approaches. Do you think the buffalo will wait for your warfare?"

Yellow Fang sat down with an angry muttering. David shivered at the fury in the look the young warrior gave the chief.

The old one who had first spoken addressed the chief. "Black Hawk is the leader of our hunts. What does he counsel?"

All eyes turned toward the chief of the Dog Soldiers, who sat near the door. Black Hawk's face was troubled.

"I know not how to answer the grandfather's question," he said slowly. "My heart lies heavy under the burden of a dream that came to me in the night, even as the Pawnees were stealing our ponies."

"Speak to us of this dream!" He-Who-Speaks-Wisely, the shaman, commanded.

Black Hawk began slowly, choosing his words with care. "I walked alone among cliffs," he remembered. "I came to a spring and bent down to the water to drink. The water was still, and I saw myself in it, yet I was not myself, for instead of my head, I had a buffalo head. I saw the horns. Then suddenly I saw other buffalo heads around my head in the water. As I gazed, a stream of blood flowed down over the earth close to my hand, wetting my hand with its red. I turned. Behind me a buffalo herd lay bleeding. From them the blood flowed." He paused, frowning.

"Is there more?" the shaman demanded.

"No more. I was awakened then by the shouts of our people."

There was silence in the tepee. Breathlessly the warriors waited, their eyes on He-Who-Speaks-Wisely. For many moments the shaman sat silent, gazing piercingly into the fire, pondering the words of Black Hawk. Then at last he arose, wrapped his white buffalo robe about him, and addressed the people.

"Wahkan-Tanka, the Great Spirit, has spoken in a dream to Black Hawk," he announced solemnly. "We must read the dream well, for if we follow not the road it leads forth, our people will suffer. I go now to the medicine tepee. There I will pray the prayers of our fathers, that we may follow the counsel of the Great Spirit without error."

There was silence in the tepee after his departure. The warriors sat motionless, eyes lowered. David stole a glance at Little Bear. His Indian brother's face was composed, withdrawn. His eyes were half closed. David looked down at the rope end in his hand. It was hard to realize that Blue Thunder was gone. There was a heavy feeling in his chest. Unless Standing Wolf and Star Watcher were successful, he would never see the gray stallion again, would never feel the playful nuzzling of the cold nose against his cheek, the quick spring of the stallion under him as they raced across the prairie. Hot tears stung his eyes. He clutched the frayed rope until his knuckles whitened.

An hour passed. Still the warriors waited in silence.

Suddenly there was the soft whisper of moccasined feet outside the tepee. The door hanging swept aside. Two braves stepped into the tepee. Their copper skins glistened with sweat. Their black eyes glittered with excitement.

Every man in the tepee gazed eagerly at the newcomers. The scouts had returned from the upper prairie.

"What word do you bring!" Strong Wind asked harshly.

"The great herd on the upper prairie has been stampeded by the Pawnees," the first scout announced. "The buffalo have run away from the enemy. They have run away from the open plain and danger, run for miles across toward the rising sun."

"The Pawnees are gone," the second scout added. "The buffalo have slowed. They are tired from their running. They will not return to the open plain beyond the hills. They are grazing straight down toward the bluffs on the hunting ground of our fathers."

Strong Wind made a sound deep in his throat. "The Great Spirit is caring for his children," he said softly. Then to the scouts, he said: "You have done well. Go to your tepees. Eat and rest before you return to your watch."

Outside the drums began to beat, swelling louder and louder. Soon the harsh sound of the rattle joined their throbbing. Suddenly the door-flap was flung back, and the shaman entered the tepee.

David gasped. In his hands the shaman bore a hollow buffalo head, curved ebony horns gleaming dully. Over one arm he carried a shaggy brown buffalo robe. Slowly he advanced until he stood facing the council.

"Hear me, my people, hear my message of hope. The Great Spirit has told me that he has chosen one among us to whom he will reveal the wisdom and the knowledge of the way of the buffalo."

Slowly the shaman turned until he stood facing Black Hawk. "Step forth, Black Hawk, the chosen one!" he commanded.

Slowly Black Hawk arose from his place close

[152]

beside the door and advanced toward the shaman.

"In a dream the Great Spirit has spoken to
you," the shaman told him. "By his words, he has
chosen you to save our people. You told that in
the water you saw your head, but that it was the
head of the buffalo." He held up the hollow buffalo head that he carried. "This is the head that
you saw. The buffalo mask used in the days of the
fathers of our fathers. Take it now, and place it
upon your head."

Slowly Black Hawk did as the shaman directed.
As the huge buffalo mask came down over his
head, David's skin tingled. Black Hawk's naked
body beneath the shaggy horned mask was a fear-
ful thing to see.

"You told that in the water you saw the heads
of many buffalo," the shaman continued. "They
were the heads of the herd that will follow you.
Here, place the robe about your shoulders. This is
the robe of the buffalo caller, used many, many
snows past, before our people had ponies."

Black Hawk had the heavy robe about his
shoulders. David wet his lips nervously. The flick-
ering firelight threw Black Hawk's distorted,
wavering shadow against the side of the tepee.

"The Great Spirit has sent the Pawnees to steal
our ponies that we may be tested for courage,"

the shaman announced solemnly. "He has spoken to Black Hawk that we may kill buffalo in the way of our fathers. To Black Hawk has been given the power of the caller. We will go at once to the bluffs on the hunting ground of our fathers. There the buffalo will await our coming. There Black Hawk will go out to meet the buffalo and call them into our trap. So, the Great Spirit has spoken."

The council tepee was soon emptied. Braves rushed back to their tepees to make ready for the move. Travois harnesses for the ponies were ripped apart and remade to fit human shoulders. Tepees came down. Feverishly the women sorted through their household goods, discarding all things heavy or useless.

The camp was a beehive. People shouted as they scurried back and forth. For the first time the tribe fully realized what the loss of their ponies meant.

Suddenly the crier appeared, pushing his way through the confusion, crying aloud that they must be off if they would reach the bluffs before sunset.

People grew frantic. Hastily they harnessed the dogs to the small travois, piling their belongings into the bull boats. The tepees of the old who had no sons were left folded on the ground.

Men and women pulled shoulder to shoulder in the travois harness as the pitiful procession moved out down the bank of the stream toward the prairie below. The old ones stumbled along in their wake, shoulders bowed beneath their heavy packs. No dogs barked. With tongues hanging out, they strained against the harness. Even the babies on their cradle boards made no sound.

David and Little Bear pulled shoulder to shoulder. Their travois dragged joltingly over bushes and boulders. David gritted his teeth against the chafing of the rawhide thongs on his shoulders. Longingly he thought of the times he and Little Bear had raced their horses down this very trail to the prairie.

They came down out of the foothills onto the prairie at last, and swung right. The wind was out of the north and biting cold. There was the sting of fine sleet in their faces.

David bent his head against the driving sleet. The cold knifed down inside his buckskin shirt. The harness cut into his shoulders. He glanced at Little Bear. The Indian boy's face was set. His lips were tight.

The travois jolted over the prairie. Despite the cold, David was sweating under the strain. His buckskin shirt clung clammily to his wet back. For the first time he thought longingly of the warm woolen jacket his grandma had made for him. He had left it behind with the wagon train. Dully he wondered who was wearing it now.

The sleet turned to snow. The flakes were small and frozen. The wind drove them in cutting sweeps down across the prairie. All along the trail people were falling out. The old ones squatted down beside their packs in the tall dead grass, heads down on their knees, shoulders hunched against the driving snow.

"They will catch up with us at the bluffs," Singing Water panted, seeing David's troubled face.

"You should rest from your heavy burden, Second Mother," David said worriedly. "Put your pack on the travois. Little Bear and I can manage."

Her black eyes softened. She smiled. "I am young yet, and strong," she said softly. "I will walk beside my sons to the bluffs."

Slowly the long line wound across the prairie, bodies leaning into the wind, people and travois covered by a thin powdering of freezing snow.

David lost all count of time. The wind cut mercilessly down out of the north, howling about them, like a living thing. They rested, struggled on, rested. Nobody spoke. Every breath was hoarded. Reaching the buffalo trap in time meant the difference between life and death.

Just when he was beginning to feel that he could not take another step forward, David glimpsed the pale curve of water ahead. They were coming to the river. He looked at Little Bear. Little Bear smiled grimly.

David felt a quick surge of warmth through his body. "We're going to make it!" he gasped hoarsely.

Little Bear nodded. "It will be better down in the river bed."

And it was. The poles of the travois swished over the gritty snow. The low bluffs cut off the wind. As the bluffs ahead loomed higher and higher, the pace quickened. They rounded a bend. Ahead David glimpsed the bleached bones that littered the river bed. He heaved a spent sigh of thanksgiving.

They pitched their tepees close up under the bluff, not far from the old buffalo pen. Little Bear and David forced their exhausted bodies down to the river bank. Men and women and children

were feverishly gathering driftwood. The two
boys set to work.

Soon smoke swirled up through the smokeholes of the tepees. The exhausted tribe settled
down for the night.

The Buffalo Come

14

At midnight the scouts rode in from the upper
prairie. The clatter of their ponies' hoofs on the
frozen snow aroused the camp. Eagerly the Indians hurried out to follow the scouts to the tepee
of Strong Wind.

Their report was terse. The buffalo had bedded
down at sunset, heads to the driving snow. Al-

ready they were beginning to mill about, pawing through the snow to reach grass. Soon they would begin to move. The tribe must make haste.

Torches were lighted. Quickly the men set to work repairing the fences of the buffalo pen at the foot of the bluff. Women and boys scurried in and out, clearing the pen of its litter of bones.

Toward morning the snow stopped. The sky in the east paled to gray. The torches were put out. The work went on.

The sun rose unseen in a leaden sky. The last log was heaved into place. The pen was ready.

The hours passed. Down beside the river the women labored, building the drying racks for the meat. At the foot of the bluff the men squatted silently on their haunches, buffalo robes tight about their shoulders, waiting for the signal from the Dog Soldiers.

David and Little Bear watched from a distance, until their feet ached with the cold. Then they returned to the tepee and sat beside the fire. Their moccasins were soaking wet from the snow. They stripped them off and hung them close to the fire to dry.

"Where was Black Hawk this morning?" David asked. "I didn't see him while we were working on the pen."

"The caller never shows himself before the

hunt, White Eagle. All night long he fasts and prays in the tepee of the shaman. Sweet grass and pine burn on the fire. Black Hawk will have purified his body in the smoke from this sacred fire. When the time comes he will put on the buffalo mask and the robe and go forth up the bluff to encounter the buffalo. This is the way of our people."

David sighed wearily. "I wonder where Standing Wolf and Star Watcher are," he murmured wistfully. "If only they steal back our horses! Blue Thunder had learned to come to my whistle. You saw him do it, Little Bear."

Little Bear did not answer. He had turned his head, ear cocked. Suddenly he grabbed his moccasins. "The drums!" he shouted. "It is the signal! The buffalo are coming!"

The boys snatched up their buffalo robes and raced for the bluff. Men and women and children crowded the trail, hurrying, straining to reach the upper prairie. On top of the bluff the Indians broke into two groups. One group ran straight down the east line. David and Little Bear raced with the others across to the west side. They dodged behind a mound close to the bluff. At each mound two or three Indians dropped out, vanishing behind the stone pile. Soon the trap was empty.

The boys crawled up the side of their mound on hands and knees, straining to see to the north. At first they saw nothing. Then suddenly Little Bear grabbed David's arm.

"Look!" he whispered hoarsely. "The buffalo. Under the frost cloud, there where the sky meets the earth."

The white frost cloud appeared unmoving. Then slowly it widened and lifted, until beneath could be seen the black line of buffalo grazing slowly toward them. The boys watched, breathing in shallow gasps.

All at once Little Bear gave a choked cry. "See!" he whispered excitedly. "That dark shape moving through the grass beyond the farthest mounds!"

David strained to see. "Where— I see it! It's—"

"It's Black Hawk!" Little Bear hissed. "Watch!"

At first the dark shape in the grass was without form, moving slowly first this way, then that. Then the massive head with its long curved horns reared up out of the grass, then the huge shaggy hump. Black Hawk stood up, stooped grotesquely under the mask and the robe. For long moments he waited, motionless, then slowly moved forward one step at a time toward the north and the grazing herd.

Every few steps the masked figure halted, sank down out of sight in the grass, then rose again, first the head, then the hump, then the whole body.

"Soon he will begin to call," Little Bear breathed.

As if in echo to his words, the voice of the caller came faintly. "Hoo, hoo, hoo," came the call, "hoo, hoo, hoo." At the same moment Black Hawk began slowly to whirl, dancing, swaying his body from side to side.

Three buffalo cows, grazing well out ahead of the herd, stopped and raised shaggy heads, staring in the direction of the caller. Black Hawk dropped down out of sight in the grass. Slowly the cows started toward him. The herd drifted after them, still grazing.

Black Hawk raised up. Deliberately he turned and started out at a walk toward the bluff. The cows followed slowly. Suddenly the lead cow broke into a trot. Black Hawk eased into a slow run. Mask and robe flopped as he matched pace with the cow.

The whole herd was trotting now. Black Hawk speeded up. The herd broke into a run. Snow sprayed out from under their hoofs. Black Hawk lengthened his stride, running straight down toward the center of the trap. With heads down and tails up, the buffalo galloped after him.

They swept down into the mouth of the trap.

The buffalo were gaining on Black Hawk. Suddenly along both sides of the trap men and women and children leaped out from behind the mounds as the buffalo thundered past, whooping and yelling and waving their robes. The buffalo panicked. Blindly they pushed and shoved toward the center as they fled from the yelling, screaming menace on both sides straight toward the bluff ahead.

Almost to the bluff Black Hawk suddenly threw robe and mask from him and whirled toward the right, racing for his life. David and Little Bear were out in front of their mound, screaming at the top of their lungs. "Run, Black Hawk! Run!"

With one last frantic burst of speed the caller cleared the outer fringe of the herd. He streaked past David and Little Bear, stumbled to a stop, and collapsed against their mound, chest heaving, body streaked with dirt and sweat.

At that moment the lead cow reached the edge of the bluff and plunged out into space. The boys stared openmouthed as she fell, turning end over end. Then over the bluff surged a bellowing, seething wave of brown backs, turning, falling. A frost cloud rolled up from the thundering herd, blotting out the bluff.

On and on they came, shaggy heads close to

the ground, running blindly, goaded to frenzy by the shrill screams of the Indians.

"There must be hundreds of them," David whispered with awe. "They're like a brown river flowing over the bluff."

Slowly the ranks thinned and the frost cloud lifted. Only a few stragglers were left in the trap. Warriors snatched up their bows and arrows from behind the mounds. The stragglers stumbled exhaustedly over the trampled earth, heads down, black tongues hanging out, flanks heaving. Arrows twanged. One by one they dropped, lifeless lumps. The hunt was over.

Already the tribe was racing toward the trail down the bluff, yelling and shouting joyfully as they hurried to the skinning and butchering.

David's stomach heaved when he caught sight of the pen. Blood flowed over the trampled snow. Great brown piles of shaggy bodies were stacked grotesquely against the bluff. Crippled buffalo bellowed frantically as they crawled across the pen, dragging their hindquarters. The braves were already inside the pen. Clubs crunched against bone as they finished off the crippled. Carcasses were dragged from the piles. Knives flashed. Hides rolled back. Women raced to peg

[165]

them to the ground before they froze stiff.

David worked grimly beside Strong Wind and Little Bear. His body was wet with sweat. His leggings were bloody to the knees. When he paused for breath the icy wind knifed down inside his clammy shirt. He shivered violently.

"Do not pause in your labor, White Eagle," Strong Wind panted, "or else the north wind will bring evil spirits into your body."

David plunged blindly back into the gore, pulling, tugging, straining as they dragged the massive carcasses across the frozen ground. He shut his ears to the feeble bellowing of dying buffalo. He shut his eyes to the flow of blood on the ground.

The sun was low in the west when Strong Wind at last bade the boys stop and catch their breath. The three leaned back against the bluff, eyes closed, bodies slack. Strong Wind was the first to recover.

"The Great Spirit has saved our tribe," he said joyfully. "Our people will not starve for lack of ponies."

David opened his eyes. The chief stood erect, gazing proudly at the mountains of red flesh piled high on the snow.

"There will be meat in the tepees until the

snows are gone from the prairie," Strong Wind added thankfully.

David straightened up away from the bluff. Somehow the shaggy brown carcasses and the piles of bloody meat no longer spelled carnage. Instead, they meant life-giving food for the people. Slowly he turned and looked up at the chief. Before the understanding in Strong Wind's dark eyes, the boy's face burned.

"There will be meat in the tepees," David echoed humbly. "Our people will not starve."

The Thank-offering Robe

15

The butchering was finished next morning. Tepees stood shrouded in heavy layers of smoke from the drying pits. Thin sheets of meat hung from the drying racks. Pegged-down hides covered the ground along the river bank from the bluff to far below the village. From the tepees drifted the tantalizing aroma of roasting hump ribs.

Yet the people made no feasts. They made no songs. They did not dance to celebrate the coming of the buffalo. There was meat in the tepees, yes, but their ponies were gone. Even the faces of little children reflected the grim look of their elders.

Braves gathered in twos and threes along the river bank, buffalo robes about their shoulders, talking furtively together. When Strong Wind walked through the village, they followed him with their eyes, somberly, expectantly.

"They are waiting for our father to call the council together," Little Bear whispered to David. "Now that the buffalo are slain, they are remembering that without ponies, our tribe is powerless before our enemies. They want ponies, and quickly."

"But what about Standing Wolf and Star Watcher?" David protested.

Little Bear beckoned David out of earshot of the others. They squatted down beside a boulder, out of the wind.

"I heard our father and mother whispering together last night while you slept," Little Bear told him. "Yellow Fang is still angry because our father shamed him before the council. He is stirring the young braves up. He taunts them into fury, laughing and jeering that they sit safely at home and let old men try to recapture our ponies."

"Can't our father stop him?" David asked in surprise. "He's the chief."

Little Bear shook his head. "Not unless the council votes with him this afternoon, and Yellow Fang has already won some of them over. The council members lost their horses, also. They, too, are desperate."

"Why does Yellow Fang call Standing Wolf and Star Watcher old men? They're not over forty years of age."

Little Bear shrugged. "They had already counted coup by the time Yellow Fang was born," he replied. "Yellow Fang has seen but twenty snows, yet already he has stolen more ponies than any man in the tribe. The long scars on his cheek he received in battle. It is a mark of honor, for he brought home the scalp of the warrior who wounded him."

"He must be brave."

"He is brave, yes, but our father says he is too reckless. He will endanger the whole tribe, just to prove his courage."

"Where is he, anyway? I haven't seen him today."

Little Bear pointed. "Up there, atop the bluff. That's Flat Nose and Long Wing and Sleeping

Owl with him." Little Bear spat. "Those three would do anything Yellow Fang told them."

"Are they keeping watch for our horses?"

"Hoping they won't come," Little Bear growled. "Yellow Fang is greedy for more scalps to hang on his lodge pole. Our father says he and his friends are organizing a raiding party. Our father says they are all hot bloods. All they crave is excitement."

Suddenly David got to his feet. "Look! Strong Wind and Black Hawk are climbing the trail up the bluff."

Little Bear jumped up. "Something is going to happen," he cried. "Come, let us hurry and follow them."

The boys raced in and out through the pegged-down hides to the foot of the trail. They caught up with Strong Wind and Black Hawk at the top of the bluff. Panting hard, they followed the two men across to where Yellow Fang stood with his friends.

"Have you come to watch with us for sight of our ponies, Strong Wind?" Yellow Fang asked mockingly.

His three friends laughed loudly. Strong Wind shook his head, ignoring the taunt.

"Standing Wolf and Star Watcher have the cunning learned from many raids," he said com-

posedly. "They will steal back our ponies, if anyone can."

"Aaah!" Yellow Fang snarled. "You told me before our people in the council tepee that I spoke
with the tongue of an infant. I say that you,
Strong Wind, now speak with the tongue of an
old woman. Standing Wolf and Star Watcher.
Old men. Both of them."

David and Little Bear stared aghast. Black
Hawk took one step forward, raising his rawhide
quirt threateningly. Strong Wind motioned him
back.

"You are young, Yellow Fang, and reckless
with the hot blood of youth," the chief said slowly.
"You are eager to show your courage in battle, to
count coup on your enemy. We know that you
are brave. You have proved that many times
over."

"I have proved my courage," Yellow Fang acknowledged sullenly. "Why do you seek me out,
Strong Wind? What do you want of me?"

"I want you to wait a little longer," Strong
Wind said frankly, "before you organize a raiding party. The sun has risen but twice since
Standing Wolf and Star Watcher departed. Give
them more time, before you persuade our young
men to join in a raiding party. Snow lies thick on

the ground. It is the worst time in the year for a war party."

Yellow Fang laughed derisively. "Strong Wind grows cautious with age," he jeered contemptuously.

"I ask you to listen, Yellow Fang," Strong Wind said sternly.

"Your voice is lost on the air, Strong Wind," Yellow Fang snarled. "Standing Wolf and Star Watcher have failed. They had but one chance—to overtake the Pawnee thieves that first night. After that their common ponies would have played out. No, we shall go."

"And what if the council forbids it?"

"Forbids?" Yellow Fang laughed mirthlessly. "Forbid is a strong word, my chief. Do not forget that our council members have lost their ponies, too. Call your council. Let them vote. You will see. When the sun sets I will put on my war shirt and leggings. I will paint my face with black and with scarlet. On my head, I will place my war bonnet of eagle feathers. I will go out through the village, singing my war song. Our young men will follow me."

Strong Wind turned on his heel and started back toward the trail, Black Hawk and the boys following.

"Little Bear and the paleface may go with our war party," Yellow Fang shouted tauntingly. "We shall need boys to tend the ponies we capture."

Strong Wind made no reply. Silently they descended the trail. At the foot the chief turned to the boys.

"Return to our tepee," he said sternly. "I go with Black Hawk to the tepee of our shaman."

All that long day the boys crouched beside the fire in the tepee, waiting and listening. Even Singing Water kept silence, as she stitched on a shirt for her husband. The sudden barking of a dog outside made them all start.

"Even the village waits, listening," Singing Water sighed. "The bark of a dog sounds loud in the silence."

Time dragged. They ate a few mouthfuls of hump ribs late in the afternoon, but without appetite.

An hour before sunset they heard voices approaching. Little Bear ran to the door and peered out. "Our father is coming," he whispered excitedly.

Strong Wind stepped inside the tepee. "Bring me my ceremonial shirt," he said shortly.

Singing Water hurried to the back of the tepee.

She brought the shirt, soft white buckskin, embroidered with dyed porcupine quills.

Strong Wind put it on. "Now, my ceremonial leggings," he told her.

"What is happening, my father?" Little Bear asked timidly.

Strong Wind laughed mirthlessly. "You will soon see, little one," he said curtly. "There will be no council meeting this day. Yellow Fang will not sing his war song in the village at sunset."

Singing Water clapped her hands softly. "I know, the shaman is to make the thank-offering. That is why you wear the ceremonial shirt."

Strong Wind nodded. For a moment, a smile quirked the corners of his mouth. "Yellow Fang will be very angry," he said complacently, "but not even he will be reckless enough to speak out against the thank-offering."

"What is this thank-offering?" David whispered to Little Bear.

At that instant the loud throbbing beat of drums started up in the distance.

"In a minute you will see," Little Bear whispered.

"Come," Strong Wind told them, and led his family out from the tepee.

From all over the village people were hurrying

toward the tepee of the shaman. David saw Yellow Fang walking slowly through the crowd with his friends.

"Look at Yellow Fang," he whispered to Little Bear as they hurried along. "His face is like thunder."

Little Bear grinned. "Our father has outwitted him," he said happily.

Before his tepee He-Who-Speaks-Wisely, the shaman, awaited the people. The old man stood straight and tall, face lifted to the sky. Across his outstretched arms lay a curly buffalo robe, so soft and glossy that it glistened in the pale sunlight. Broad bands of dyed porcupine quills were sewed around the edges. David caught his breath at its beauty.

"What is it?" he whispered to Little Bear.

"Shh. It is our thank-offering to the Great Spirit for good hunting," his Indian brother breathed.

The whole tribe had gathered. Solemnly the shaman wheeled and set out toward the trail up the bluff, the drummers and the people following. They reached the foot of the trail. The drums muted. The voice of the shaman rose in a solemn chant.

The day has come,
The hour is sunset,

We climb to the crest of the hill,
We turn our faces to the sinking sun in
the west,
We bear our thank-offering to the
Great Spirit!

One by one the people joined in the chanting until the bluff echoed back their solemn voices. Slowly the procession moved up the trail, chanting loudly, chanting softly. David walked silently beside Little Bear. His skin prickled at the rising, falling cadences of the Indians' voices.

The procession came out onto the upper prairie. The shaman led the way across to the high ridge on the east. Chanting and swaying, the long line wound its way up the ridge.

They reached the top and halted, facing west. They fell silent. David slowly turned his head. The village was hidden by the bluff. The smoke from the drying pits hung heavy in the clear cold air, blotting out the river at the foot of the bluff. Beyond the smoke the pale water gleamed in the distance. The boy sighed longingly. The prairie stretched away still and empty as far as eye could see.

All at once the drums stilled. David looked at the shaman. The old man stood on the highest point of the ridge, his body silhouetted against the crimson and purple of the sunset. Slowly he raised the buffalo robe high toward the setting sun. His voice rose rich and deep.

> *Hear thy people, Wahkan-Tanka,*
> *You have given us good hunting—*
> *In the midst of our tribulations,*
> *You have sent us the buffalo.*
> *You have spared thy people from*
> *   starvation.*
> *Accept this thank-offering for*
> *   thy goodness.*
> *Accept the thanks of thy people.*

He stooped and spread out the glossy robe over a low hummock. As he straightened up, the drums began to beat. Silently the people turned away to return down the trail to the village.

David turned to follow. All at once he felt hard fingers dig into his arm. It was Little Bear. His Indian brother stood gazing past him out over the bluff and the smoke of the village.

"What is it?" David asked. "What are you looking at?"

Little Bear did not reply. He stood squinting into the glare of pale sunlight on the river. Suddenly he gave a great shout. The people turned, startled.

"The horses! The horses!" Little Bear screamed, pointing toward the south. "The horses! The horses!"

The Scalp Dance

16

Men and women and children pelted down the trail to the foot of the bluff. Laughing and shouting, they surged down through the village, past the last pegged-down buffalo hides, and around the bend in the river.

Suddenly they brought up short, fell silent. As far as eye could see, their horses stood in a line along the river, heads down, drinking. Standing Wolf and Star Watcher rode slowly up along the line toward the people. Strong Wind stepped out from the crowd and advanced to meet them.

David and Little Bear stood on tiptoe, craning their necks to see. David's throat ached with excitement. Where was Blue Thunder?

"Come! Up on top of the bank," Little Bear hissed.

They scrambled up the sandy bank. David's gaze swept down the line of horses. He gave a choked sigh. He had glimpsed a gray head flung up, a long black mane streaming in the wind.

"I see Fleet Deer," Little Bear whispered excitedly, "and Hoofs-That-Flash, our father's runner, and there—there beyond is Blue Thunder."

David nodded wordlessly, blinking back tears.

Below, chief and warriors met. Standing Wolf and Star Watcher reined up their ponies. Strong Wind raised his hand in greeting.

"Welcome, my warriors. You have returned to your people as heroes. You have stolen our ponies back from the Pawnees, our enemies. Great honor you have brought upon yourselves and your families."

"All this we have done," Standing Wolf told him, "and more. We have slain our enemies with our knives as they lay sleeping, but before we

killed them, we touched them with our hands.
We count coup upon seven. Star Watcher three,
and I, Standing Wolf, four."

A low exulting roar welled up from the crowd
as Standing Wolf's hand fumbled at his waist for
a moment, then came up, holding aloft by their
stiff black scalp locks a cluster of Pawnee scalps.

David peered through the thickening twilight
as Standing Wolf waved the scalps in triumph.
The wild shouts of the people were not so loud as
the drumming in his ears. He swallowed convulsively, fighting the wave of nausea that welled up
within him.

Little Bear was jumping up and down, screaming with joy. "Perhaps Standing Wolf will give us
a scalp lock for trimming for our shirts," he cried.

David gave him a sick smile, swallowing hard.
Below them the people were rushing forward to
claim their ponies. Little Bear leaped down the
bank.

"Hurry, White Eagle. Let us go claim our runners."

David made no move to follow, as Little Bear
darted through the crowd. Instead, he stuck two
fingers in his mouth and whistled piercingly. He
saw Blue Thunder's head go up. He whistled
again. The gray stallion wheeled. Again, the
whistle. Blue Thunder leaped forward. People

scattered before him. The stallion veered away from the river. His muscles bunched. With one long arching jump, he was on top of the bank. The drumming of his hoofs was loud in the air.

Ten feet away from the boy the stallion dug his hoofs in and slid to a stop, ears pricking forward and back. He whinnied eagerly. David ran to him. He threw his arms around the proud arched neck, running his hands over the shaggy gray coat, murmuring brokenly. "You've come back. I've missed you so much."

Boy and stallion stood together quietly, while below in the dusk Indians shouted and laughed as they drove their ponies toward the village. Carefully David ran his hands over the stallion's powerful legs, the rump, the sides.

"Nobody hurt you," he murmured thankfully. "There's not a scratch on you."

Gathering a handful of mane in his hand, the boy leaped onto the stallion's back. Slowly they moved through the twilight toward the tepee of Strong Wind.

Fires burned in the village that night. Torches flared. The air was heavy with the spicy fragrance of cedar smoke and the aroma of roasting meat.

After the feasting, men and women and children gathered in the great center circle for the chanting and the dancing. There came the loud throbbing beat of the drums, slow at first, then faster and faster. One by one the warriors began a solemn chant, their bodies swaying slowly in the light of the leaping fires.

Suddenly the women were inside the circle, bearing the seven scalps tied to long poles. They began to circle, bending and stomping in the steps of the scalp dance, the dangling scalps dipping and bobbing at the ends of the poles.

David stood beside Little Bear in the midst of the chanting, swaying men. He could not tear his gaze away from the bobbing scalps. As the crowd's frenzy mounted, he closed his eyes, but could not shut out the image of the scalps. His palms were wet with sweat. Determinedly he pressed his trembling hands hard against his thighs, but it was no use. Noiselessly he turned and crept away, stumbling blindly through the crowd.

Behind the first tepee, he was violently sick. When it was over, he staggered weakly up through the village until he reached the horses picketed before the tepee of Strong Wind. He threw his arms around Blue Thunder's neck and pressed his hot face against the shaggy mane.

Strong Wind found him there. The chief came

[184]

up so silently that he startled David. The boy swung about, straightening his shoulders as he met the chief's gaze in the light of the torch Strong Wind held aloft.

Strong Wind stooped, stuck the torch into the ground, straightened up. "My second son left the dancing," he said slowly. "Does a thing trouble White Eagle?"

Contrition touched the boy. "It was nothing, Second Father," he stammered, "only, all of a sudden I felt outside of everything, a stranger. I couldn't stop thinking of the old mother back home in my tepee, and of the brother of my father, who must have returned from the war-path by now. I know they mourn for me."

Strong Wind nodded. "It is right that you think of the old ones, White Eagle."

"My people have a word, homesickness," the boy went on. "It means that a man far away from his tepee begins to long for his people. I guess I'm homesick, that's all."

"You say 'my people,' White Eagle," Strong Wind said gently, placing a hand on the boy's shoulder. "I have watched you since your coming, Second Son. You have never forgotten your people."

The boy hung his head. "I guess not," he muttered. Then his head came up, and he met the chief's look squarely. "But I've been happy here with you and with my adopted people," he said honestly. "You have been a real father to me, Strong Wind. And Singing Water, a mother. I love you both, and Little Bear, my brother. I'll love you till the day I die!"

"You are our son, White Eagle," Strong Wind said gently. "You will ever be our second son, the brother of Little Bear. Turn this thing over in your mind, my son. When the snows are melted, and the buffalo return once more to the prairie, speak to me freely. If it is in your heart then to return to your people, we will help you."

Return to Fort Laramie

17

Day after day the snow fell. Prairie and canyons lay deep under the glistening blanket. At night the wind howled mournfully around the tepees. Out on the prairie small bands of stray buffalo, caught by the blizzard, wallowed through the deep snowdrifts, bawling, falling, struggling to their feet, staggering blindly on, seeking shelter.

Men and boys went out from the village on snowshoes, running alongside the floundering buffalo, dropping them with their arrows. The robes were in prime condition. From dawn to dusk the women worked beside the fires at the tanning. At night the heady aroma of roasting meat filled the village. There was feasting and dancing.

The stacks of robes in the tepee of Strong Wind grew higher and higher. Even when the other hunters rested, content with their winter's take, Little Bear and David went out each day with bows and arrows.

"Let them stay by the fire," Little Bear panted one morning as he and David heaved and tugged a fat cow into position for skinning. "You and I must take many robes to Fort Laramie when the snow melts, White Eagle."

David rested a moment, wiping the sweat from his forehead with mittened hand. "Well, we're getting them," he panted. "This makes five in the last two days."

Little Bear pulled out his knife and deftly ringed the cow's neck up close under the curling horns. Then he slipped the blade in under the skin at the throat and slit the skin down along the belly to the root of the tail.

"I shall need many robes to trade for a thunderstick and black powder," he said grimly, "and you will need many for the saddle for Blue Thunder. Now, while the snow lies deep and we can hunt for ourselves, is the time for us to get them."

The snows ceased. For long months the prairie lay white and glistening under the ice-crusted drifts. Even the river lay frozen. Men and boys trudged to the foothills on snowshoes and hauled back forage on sleds for the ponies.

Then suddenly one day the first slight thaw came. As the days passed the sun sent zigzag cracks through the ice. The snow on the prairie turned mushy. Snowshoes were useless. The ice on the river broke up and was swept whirling and tossing downstream in the first runoff.

Only thin patches of snow were left in the hollows on the prairie. Tender green grass carpeted the plain. At sunset one evening long V's of wild geese were seen winging swiftly northward through the sky, their hoarse honking wafting back faint and eerie.

"The wild geese seek their home beneath the north star," Strong Wind announced to his people. "It is time for us to journey southward to Fort Laramie. When the dawn comes we shall set out for our summer camp on the prairie."

David's heart hammered as he labored that

night beside Singing Water and Little Bear, packing and stacking the buffalo robes. Carefully he selected his two finest robes. One he presented to Singing Water.

"It will keep you warm and dry when the snows come again, Second Mother," he said shyly. "Remember then White Eagle, your second son, who loves you."

Singing Water stroked the glossy robe with delight. "I will remember," she promised softly, blinking tears back. "The other robe is for the old mother in your tepee beneath the rising sun," she guessed.

David nodded. "I aim to bring Grandma west, soon as I can," he told her. "You and she would get along fine."

That night, David could not sleep. For hours he tossed and turned on his buffalo robe. At last he got up and slipped to the back of the tepee and fumbled out the little Testament from his shoulder pouch. Taking it back to his bed, he snuggled down, cheek against the little book. Happily he thought of riding Blue Thunder into Fort Laramie. And after that, the long journey home. His eyelids drooped. "Grandma," he murmured drowsily, and was asleep.

Singing Water routed them out before dawn.

Outside, all was noisy confusion. Dogs barked. Horses whinnied. People shouted. Tepees came down. Pack ponies and travois were loaded. Women sang as they worked. All were happy to be on the move at last.

The scouts had ridden on ahead. The old men had made their pipe offering to the Great Spirit. Already they had disappeared beyond the bend in the river.

One by one the families found their places in the procession. Braves raced their ponies up and down the line, keeping order. As the last travois lurched out across the sand, the warriors of the rear guard fell into place behind the cavalcade.

David and Little Bear rode with Strong Wind and Singing Water at the head of the procession. The boys wheeled their runners in and out, keeping the pack ponies in line.

At last the procession climbed up out of the river bed and stretched out for over a mile across the lower prairie. Ponies settled down. People laughed and shouted to one another. The sun was warm on their backs. They were headed for their summer home.

All that day they traveled across the rolling plain, stopping for the night beside a swollen muddy stream. The ponies were hobbled and turned loose to graze, but the horse guard was doubled. Strong Wind forbade fires. Sentinels circled the camp all night. The stars still twinkled palely in the sky next morning when they pushed on.

"Do Strong Wind and the Dog Soldiers fear the Pawnees?" David murmured to Little Bear as they rode knee to knee through the dark before dawn.

"Until we cross the Platte, there is always danger," Little Bear told him. "We have many robes and our ponies. Besides, the Pawnees lost seven warriors to Standing Wolf and to Star Watcher. This, they will not have forgotten."

David shivered. There was still over three days' hard travel before they would reach Fort Laramie.

They crossed the Cheyenne on the morning of the third day. Their trail led straight south. Mile after mile the caravan crept between low hills. They were following a wide sandy channel winding in and around hills. Clouds of dust billowed up from under the horses' hoofs. The sun blazed down. There was no breeze.

They reached a straight stretch of trail between the hills. Strong Wind sent two scouts ahead.

"Search the hills," he ordered brusquely. "Every hill could hide a war party of Pawnees. Every clump of sagebrush, every piñon could hide an enemy warrior. Don't spare your ponies. Make haste. Return by the nooning."

The scouts galloped away. David watched until they disappeared back of a hill. Puffs of dust kicked up by their ponies still hung in the air. The boy gazed uneasily at the hills. He shivered.

Now the pace quickened. Travois jounced over the rocks that lay loose on the trail. Babies whimpered. Mothers shushed them sternly. No one talked. There was an urgency to their movement.

The sun was past the zenith when Strong Wind at last called the nooning halt. People dismounted, resting their ponies. David and Little Bear munched hungrily at the pemmican which Singing Water handed them. Strong Wind was standing a little apart from the others, with Standing Wolf and Yellow Fang. Still munching, the boys edged through the crowd toward them.

"I like it not that our scouts have not returned," they heard Strong Wind say as they approached. "Our tribe is in danger. I have heard nothing, seen nothing, yet in my very bones I feel a foreboding, a warning. You, Yellow Fang, double the guards on the left flank. And you, Standing Wolf, do the same on the right. Keep your warriors within a hundred yards of the caravan. Watch the hills." His voice deepened, rang out. "Do not take your eyes from the hills! Until we are out on the open plain, I shall know no peace!"

They pushed on, flanked by the doubled guards. Mile after mile fell behind them. Still the scouts did not return. Strong Wind had sent the old men who led the procession back to ride on travois. Now the chief rode alone at the head of the line, his face impassive, his eyes scanning the hills.

The sun sank low in the west. The long line wound around the base of a sprawling hill. All at once Strong Wind called a halt. David and Little Bear rode forward beside him. The chief had reined up on the rim of a wide dry wash. Somberly he gazed across at the trail they must follow. Half a mile beyond the wash to the south a large steep hill rose high above the prairie. To the west of the hill a grove of cottonwoods marked the curving banks of a creek.

Yellow Fang and Standing Wolf galloped up from the flanks. Star Watcher and Black Hawk rode up from the caravan. The boys reined their horses back as the five men bunched their ponies close and talked together.

"What do you think they're powwowing about?" David asked uneasily.

"Darkness will fall soon," Little Bear told him.

"They must find a spot near water to pitch our tepees, a place that will give us protection from attack."

They watched the men. There was much shaking of heads, much waving of arms. Finally, Star Watcher wheeled his pony and galloped back to the caravan, returning shortly with two scouts. The scouts edged their ponies into the huddle. There was more talking. At last the scouts reined back from the others and sent their ponies down into the dry wash. They vanished for a second, then they scrambled out up the far side. There, the scouts swung west toward the long line of cottonwoods at a fast gallop. Their ponies left a long trail of dust hanging in the air.

Strong Wind and the four warriors sat watching. The boys rode up beside them. Yellow Fang was talking.

"If you are right, Strong Wind—if the Pawnees are really near by—our scouts should find their tracks."

"Unless they have laid a trap," the chief replied darkly. "Since the sun rose this morning, I have felt this foreboding. Why else did our scouts not return at the nooning? They have been slain by our enemies. I have a foreboding that the Pawnees lie hidden somewhere near by, waiting for us to walk into their trap."

David licked his lips nervously. He glanced across the plain. The scouts had vanished into the cottonwoods. The boy turned and stared at the high hill in front of them. With trembling fingers he checked his rifle that lay across his knees.

The minutes passed. No one spoke. The horses shifted comfortably, heads drooping, tails switching. Suddenly Little Bear uttered a sharp cry.

"They are returning!" he called excitedly, pointing toward the cottonwoods.

The scouts raced their ponies back across the plain, dust billowing up in their wake. They crossed the dry wash. They reined up before the chief.

"No one has been near the creek for many suns," the first scout reported positively.

"We rode around back of the big hill there," the second said, pointing. "We found no tracks, no signs."

Strong Wind sighed. "There is no other place for us to camp," he said heavily. "Call up your warriors, Yellow Fang. Cross the wash. Station them between the caravan and the big hill. Watch the hill!"

When Yellow Fang had the left-flank guard across the wash and in a tight group facing the hill, Strong Wind gave the signal for the tribe to move forward. Down and up out of the dry wash the long line moved slowly. There was little noise. The soft whinny of a pony sounded loud in the silence.

David crossed the wash with Strong Wind and Little Bear. They reined up on the side. Slowly the caravan wound past, angling west, toward the cottonwoods.

Under his knees David felt Blue Thunder's muscles ripple nervously. He patted the stallion's neck. There was a tenseness in the air. The thud of his own heartbeat sounded loud in the boy's ears. Slowly his gaze swept the plain, passed over the bobbing heads in the caravan, came to rest at the foot of the high hill. Slowly he raised his eyes up over boulders and piñon. Suddenly his heart stopped. Silhouetted against the blue sky atop the hill was a long line of dark specks. He blinked his eyes. They were still there. Horse heads! Lances! War bonnets!

"Strong Wind!" he screamed. "On top of the hill. Pawnees! Pawnees!"

Surprise Attack

18

"Pawnees!" David screamed again. "Pawnees!"

The caravan froze. Over the crest of the hill rode a wide straight line of warriors, fifty strong, their chief riding before them on a snow white pony. Just under the crest they halted, sunlight flashing on raised lances. Like carven images, they waited.

Strong Wind's shrill, outdrawn "A-i-i-e-e!" shrieked across the plain. At that instant the line of Pawnees shifted, split into two halves.

"Women and children back into the wash with the ponies!" Strong Wind shouted. "Little Bear. White Eagle. Pass the word along. Back into the wash!"

The plain was a wild confusion of running children, plunging horses, struggling women. The left half of the Pawnee line was racing down toward them in single file. On the plain Yellow Fang screamed his bloodcurdling war cry and led his warriors to meet the enemy.

David and Little Bear clung grimly to their plunging horses as the screaming women surged around them down into the wash. The Pawnee line was almost down to the plain. Yellow Fang's warriors had halted, lances raised, arrows drawn.

Suddenly the line of Pawnees swung out to the right in a wide arc. David's heart thudded. They were going to cut Yellow Fang and his warriors off from the rest.

At that instant the second group of Pawnees charged down the hill in an unbroken line straight toward Yellow Fang and his men. Strong Wind was lashing his pony across the plain toward where Standing Wolf and his warriors were guarding the rear of the fleeing tribe. Suddenly the chief turned his head, saw Yellow Fang's peril. He reined his pony back on its haunches.

"Bring your warriors!" he shouted to Standing Wolf. Wheeling his pony, he raced toward Yellow Fang.

He was too late. The line of screaming Pawnees swept between him and the warriors. Dust billowed up. The air was loud with the whining twang of arrows. Horses screamed. Strong Wind rode low on the neck of his pony straight into the inferno. Behind him thundered Standing Wolf and his warriors.

Suddenly Strong Wind's pony leaped out into the clear. Strong Wind lay slumped over his neck.

"Father!" Little Bear screamed.

"He's wounded," David shouted. "He's falling."

Strong Wind's pony staggered, stopped, head hanging. Slowly the chief's body slipped lower and lower, fell clear. At that instant a white pony darted out from the battle. It was the Pawnee chief. His lance was poised. He drove his pony straight toward the fallen Strong Wind.

Little Bear screamed and lashed Fleet Deer into a run out across the plain. David jerked Blue Thunder to the left. He had the Pawnee chief in the clear. He raised his rifle, sighted. The rifle cracked. The Pawnee chief's hands flew up. The lance fell from his grasp. He tumbled backwards off the white pony.

Two Pawnee warriors galloped to him, scooped his body up, and raced away. The Pawnees were thrown into confusion. They began a ragged retreat toward the hill. The battle was over.

Dusk was falling. Across the plain the retreating Pawnees vanished back of the big hill. Sioux women wailed mournfully as they bore in those fallen in the fight. Four wounded. Three dead. Yellow Fang was dead, a hero in battle.

Down in the wash the shaman worked feverishly over Strong Wind. An arrow had gone through the chief's shoulder, close above the heart. Now the blood was staunched. Chanting the wail for the wounded, the shaman bandaged the wounds.

Weakly the chief raised his head from the buffalo robe where they had laid him. His eyes found Singing Water and the boys, where they crouched close by, watching.

"Our sons are now warriors," he whispered proudly. "They have dared the arrows of our enemies. White Eagle has slain the chief of the war party. They have both counted coup." His eyes closed. His head sank back.

David shuddered. From the distance came the wailing lamentations of the widows of the dead warriors. Strong Wind opened his eyes.

"The fight is not yet over," he gasped weakly. "When the sun rises, the Pawnees will return."

Night fell. Black Hawk and Standing Wolf conferred briefly with Strong Wind. Then Black Hawk called the people together.

"Throw up barricades along the wash," he cried loudly. "Use the bundles of buffalo hides. Drag back the ponies killed in the fight. Use the travois, logs, anything, but make haste. We must be done before dawn."

Feverishly they labored through the long night, warriors alongside women and children, fumbling and stumbling in the darkness, no one speaking, no one resting. From across the plain came the faint throbbing of Pawnee war drums, the flicker of fires.

"There are too many fires," David heard Black Hawk tell Standing Wolf as he stumbled past them in the dark. "They have brought up many warriors from their camp."

The boy had little time to think as he and Little Bear dragged bundle after bundle of buffalo hides up out of the wash. His hands bled from the rawhide ropes. His chest ached.

The sky was graying in the east when they were finished. The crude barricade stretched waist high between the wash and the plain. Black Hawk galloped along outside the breastwork.

"Women and children down into the wash," he shouted. "Warriors, take your places. Spread out. Stretch the line. String your bows. Look to your arrows."

David and Little Bear crouched down together near the center of the line. David rested his rifle across a bundle of hides. He spread out balls and patches, laid out his powder horn.

"String your bow, White Eagle," Little Bear said excitedly. "You may need it, once the fighting begins."

David obeyed. His fingers shook as he bent the bow.

All at once someone slipped in beside them.

"My father," Little Bear cried. "With you beside us, we shall beat off our foe."

"Strong Wind," David exclaimed in dismay. "You'll break open your wounds."

Strong Wind shook his head. His eyes were sunken. His face was drawn with suffering. "The place of a chief is beside his warriors, Second Son," he said hoarsely, stringing his bow with trembling fingers. "Our men will have strong hearts with their chief fighting beside them."

David said nothing more. He crouched behind the barricade, peering through the mist that shrouded the plain. His heart was hammering. Resolutely he shut away thoughts of his Grandma and Uncle Andrew and home.

The eastern sky was streaked with red. Slowly the mist lifted. David's breath caught in his throat. Across the plain at the foot of the hill were the Pawnees. Twice as many as the day before. Their ponies were drawn up in a long line. They were moving out.

"They will make a run past us from the west," Strong Wind said grimly. "Take care, my sons. They will ride fast. Aim at their ponies."

David wet his lips nervously as the long line of Pawnees galloped out single file in a wide arc to their left. He picked up his rifle without taking his eyes from the blurred streak of ponies and riders now outlined against the cottonwoods in the distance. Suddenly he stiffened.

"Look!" he cried. "They're stopping."

The racing line of Pawnees had faltered. Ponies hunkered back on their haunches. The line was breaking up.

There came a heavy rumble, like distant thunder. A cloud of dust rolled out from back of the high hill. There was the muffled crack of a dozen rifles. Suddenly a solid brown wave of buffalo poured out from back of the hill and rolled down toward the Pawnee warriors.

Pawnee ponies reared, screaming, and lunged out across the plain in front of the onrushing buffalo. The panicked buffalo raced headlong out across the plain. Pawnees and buffalo swept down past the east end of the Sioux barricade.

On and on plunged the endless stream of maddened animals. The Sioux watched, transfixed. Over the thunder of hoofs sounded the muffled cracks of rifles. Suddenly through the cloud of dust rolling up from under the buffalo David glimpsed riders racing along on the edge of the stampede.

"Hunters!" he screamed. "White hunters." His voice was lost in the thunder of hoofs.

The plunging brown mass was past the barricade, sweeping on and on down the plain toward the east. The crack of rifles faded in the distance. Slowly the dust settled. The trampled plain stretched empty but for the huge brown carcasses fallen to the guns of the hunters.

Women and children swarmed up the banks of the wash. Still dazed by their narrow escape, the Sioux stared after the dust cloud that rolled away to the east.

Strong Wind stood leaning weakly against the barricade. "The white hunters have saved our tribe," he cried exultantly. "They have scattered our enemy. The Pawnees will not return."

Singing Water went to him, a rawhide water-bag in her hands. He drank.

"You will rest now?" she murmured pleadingly.

He shook his head impatiently, shading his eyes with his hand. "I see riders," he called to the people. "The white hunters are returning. We must make them good presents."

David and Little Bear climbed to the top of the barricade. Far down to the east they could see the hunters galloping toward them. David's heart thudded against his ribs. He jumped to the ground. White men.

Closer and closer the hunters came. David could see their buckskin suits, their flat hats. Mountain men.

As the hunters approached, Strong Wind led the people out to meet them.

"Come, White Eagle," Little Bear urged, "let us welcome the white hunters at the side of our father."

"You go on," David muttered, not understanding his own reluctance.

Little Bear wormed his way through the crowd. David's heart hammered as the white men reined up before Strong Wind. Covertly he peered at their bearded faces. There was a red beard among them. Even his Uncle Andrew's beard was no redder than that one.

He could not hear the talk. Then the hunters dismounted, and he could no longer see. Slowly he edged forward through the crowd. Suddenly he heard a man's voice, full and deep, and with a touch of Scotch burr.

"We come from Fort Laramie. We look for white boy. Son of my brother. White boy run away from fort last summer. Men at fort say he lives with tribe of Chief Strong Wind."

David froze. Blood pounded in his ears. He opened his mouth, but no sound came. He licked his lips. He tried again, but could manage only a croak. All at once he was pushing and shoving his way through the crowd. He found his voice.

"Uncle Andrew!" he screamed. "Uncle Andrew!"

The crowd parted. The red-bearded man and the boy faced each other across a dozen feet. Slowly the man's startled eyes swept down over the boy's yellow braids, the dirty face, the naked, sunburned body, the breechclout.

"David," he cried wonderingly. "David. Thank God, you're alive."

He held out his arms. David ran to him. He

clung to his uncle. "Uncle Andrew, Uncle Andrew," he sobbed over and over.

Andrew Duncan patted his nephew's head awkwardly. "You nearly scared the living daylights out of your Grandma and me, lad. Disappearing like you did."

David leaned back against his uncle's arm. "How did you get here?" he stammered. "How did you know where to look for me? Where's Grandma? Why—"

"Wait a minute, lad," his uncle interrupted laughingly. "One thing at a time. How'd I know where to look? That's easy. Old Amos told me."

"Amos," the boy echoed incredulously. "But Amos went—"

Andrew Duncan shook his head. "Amos didn't go nowhere. When you ran off, Amos up and quit his job with Bart. He's been herding horses at the fort all winter, waiting for you to show up."

David's eyes flashed. "I'm glad Amos quit Bart. Bart's rotten, Uncle Andrew. He beat me up, just for helping Little Bear. And then, when Strong Wind gave me a stallion, Bart knocked me down and took the horse away from me."

Andrew's face darkened. "I heard about it," he said grimly. "One of these days I'll get my hands on Bart Clements."

David shivered. "I don't ever want to see him

again," he said vehemently. He caught his uncle by the hand and drew him toward Strong Wind, who stood watching with Singing Water and Little Bear. "You've already met Strong Wind, Uncle Andrew, but I want you to know if it hadn't been for him, I don't know what would of become of me. He and Singing Water and Little Bear took me in. They treated me like a son. I love them like my own family."

Andrew Duncan stepped forward. Gravely he shook hands with the chief and his family. "Thanks, Chief Strong Wind," he said sincerely, "and you, ma'am, and you, Little Bear. You made good medicine for David."

Strong Wind smiled. "White hunters make good medicine for our people. White hunters save our tribe. We make present of ponies to white hunters."

"I'd sure settle for that big gray down in the wash," one of the mountain men grinned.

"No," David cried hotly. "That's Blue Thunder. Strong Wind gave him to me. Watch."

He stuck two fingers to his mouth and gave a shrill whistle. There was a sudden clatter of hoofs, an excited whinny, and the gray stallion came lunging up out of the wash. He raced across toward the boy, black mane flying. Ten feet away he dug his hoofs in and slid to a stop.

David ran to him. He threw his arms around Blue Thunder's neck. "See, Uncle Andrew. Now you know why I couldn't let Bart take him."

The mountain men crowded around the stallion admiringly. One of them fished a pouch of tobacco out of his pocket and offered it to Strong Wind. The chief took it and sniffed it appreciatively.

"Come," he said to his guests. "We rest. We smoke. Fresh buffalo meat out there on plain. Women make feast."

Cooking fires crackled outside the barricade. Hump ribs sizzled close to the flames. The white hunters sat with the council. The pipe passed from hand to hand.

David and Little Bear sat between Andrew Duncan and Strong Wind. David fidgeted as his uncle pulled deliberately on the long pipe, then passed it to Standing Wolf. He tugged at Andrew's sleeve.

"What about Grandma?" he asked. "When did you get back from Texas? Folks at home tried to make us believe you were dead. How long since you saw Grandma? Was she all right? Did she miss me?"

"Whoa, lad," Andrew laughed. "Grandma's

fine. Leastways, she was when we rode out from the fort yesterday."

It took a moment for the boy to grasp his meaning. David's mouth dropped open. "Yesterday," he gasped. "You mean Grandma's at Fort Laramie?"

Andrew nodded. "Riding herd on the prettiest bunch of longhorns you ever laid your eyes on. Course, old Amos's helping her."

David gaped at his uncle. "Grandma at Fort Laramie," he breathed.

His uncle took pity on him. "Lad, soon as I got my army discharge down in Texas, I blew my pay on a bunch of longhorns. Me and your Grandma drove them out with the first wagon train headed west. Found old Amos at Fort Laramie, and you know the rest."

Slowly David digested the news. "I still can't believe it," he whispered. "Grandma and Amos at Fort Laramie." He gave his uncle a sharp look. "What about those longhorns, Uncle Andrew? You aiming for us to go on to Oregon?"

Andrew took the pipe that Strong Wind held out to him. He took a couple of puffs, blowing smoke lazily through his nostrils.

"Well, now, David, I reckon Oregon's a mighty fine country," he said slowly, "but me, I like it

[211]

around here. Been dickering with the army a little. They'll take all the beef we can raise for them." He leaned forward and looked across at Strong Wind. "I've been hoping maybe Chief Strong Wind would help us find a good piece of range land not too far from the fort."

David looked incredulously from his uncle to Strong Wind. The chief was smiling broadly. Suddenly the boy became conscious of Little Bear's soft chuckle beside him. "You pitch tepee close to fort, White Eagle, we can hunt buffalo together."

David grinned at him. "You bet your life, we will." He grabbed Little Bear's hand and squeezed it hard. Slowly he gazed about him. Beside the cooking fire Singing Water was turning the roasting meat. He caught her eye. She smiled. Warmth flooded through him. They had been so good to him. He could never be an Indian, yet his heart had ached at the thought of parting from them forever. Now, he need not.

The sun beat down, warm on his body. Out on the plain children chased in and out, laughing and shouting as they played. Fleecy clouds drifted slowly across the blue sky. Tears of happiness stung the boy's eyes. Tomorrow he would ride into Fort Laramie on Blue Thunder, an outcast no longer, but a man proved in battle, a buffalo hunter bringing his robes to the fort for barter. In his arms he would carry the robe saved for his Grandma. She would be watching and waiting, she and old Amos.

With the back of his hand the boy dried his eyes. "Grandma," he whispered. "Tomorrow."

Glossary

BREECHCLOUT: a garment worn by Indians. The breechclout hangs from a belt around the waist, passes between the legs, and falls down from the front and rear of the belt.

BULL BOAT: a circular, basketlike boat made of woven willow sticks and covered with buffalo skins. Used for ferrying streams.

CAP: a percussion cap that replaced the flintlock on muzzle-loading rifles.

CAVVY: a band of extra mules, horses, and oxen used for replacement on wagon trains. The cavvy was driven behind the wagon train.

COUP: a brave deed or victory over one's enemy. The bravest deed was touching the enemy with bare hand or with weapon before killing him.
(Counting coup: the taking of credit for victory over an enemy, or the relating of deeds of bravery.)

DOG SOLDIERS: a tribe's bravest warriors, who act as a police force and also as officers in charge of tribal buffalo hunts.

DRYING RACK: pole frames from which buffalo meat was hung in thin strips for drying, either in sunlight or over drying pit fires.

GEE AND HAW: commands used in guiding teams without reins. Gee: to turn to off side, or to the right. Haw: to turn to the near side, or to the left.

LONG REIN: a long bridle rein, one end of which is looped around lower jaw of horse, the other end tucked into belt of rider.

GLOSSARY

PATCH (sometimes called wadding): a greased linen patch cupped around rifle ball to make it fit snugly into muzzle of rifle.

PEMMICAN: a nourishing food made of dried buffalo meat pounded into paste and mixed with melted marrow fat. Usually dried fruit or berries added.

QUIRT: A riding whip with a short handle and a lash of braided rawhide.

SHAMAN: a priest or medicine man. One wise in healing and in the interpretation of dreams.

THUNDERSTICK: an Indian term for rifle.

TRAVOIS: a V-shaped litter fashioned of two poles with platform or net between to carry baggage. These poles were attached by harness to horses or dogs, and the ends of the poles dragged on the ground.

WAHKAN-TANKA: The Great Spirit. The Indian deity.

ABOUT THE AUTHORS

Gus Tavo is the pseudonym for Martha and Gustave Ivan of Kilgore, Texas.

Mr. Ivan was born in Budapest, Hungary, and his interest in buffalo dates from the day when he saw Buffalo Bill's Great Wild West Show as a boy in that far-off city. As a youngster, Mr. Ivan had also thrilled to the Hungarian translations of James Fenimore Cooper and remembers especially the buffalo stampede in "The Prairie."

After Mr. Ivan came to the United States he worked mostly as a mural painter, travelling extensively through this country. Eventually, he became an art professor at Kilgore College where he met and married the chairman of the English Department. He is now retired and devotes his time to the painting of western and wildlife subjects. Mrs. Ivan is, at present, the Director of Guidance and Counseling at Kilgore College.

Mr. and Mrs. Ivan spend most of their summers in northern New Mexico. They often visit Clayton and watch the herd of buffalo that are part of the reconstructed stockade built by the ranchers and business men of this town.

The Ivans have again collaborated on *"The Buffalo are Running,"* as they did on their first, highly successful book, *"Hunt the Mountain Lion."*

COMPOSED, PRINTED AND BOUND BY
H. Wolff, NEW YORK.
TYPOGRAPHY BY *Tere LoPrete*